Unscripted Nights

Raw Girl x Engineer – A Story That Was Never Meant to Be Told

Volume 1

NOMAD ROSH

An Unethical Traveller

INDIA • SINGAPORE • MALAYSIA

Prologue

The Unwritten Life

Some lives are drawn with straight lines. Mine was a map of zigzags, pauses, and sudden flights.

Born into the world of machines and dreams, I chased the highest mountains. I studied Mechanical Engineering, fought through the brutal gates of IITs — made it, lost it, and wore the scars proudly.

A lifetime student of IIT Jodhpur, I carried the weight of expectations and the fire of rebellion inside me.Indian Railways gave me my first taste of power. The Ministry of Defence opened doors most could only imagine. Michelin Tyres — the German multinational giant — stamped another badge on my resume.Research papers stacked neatly. Projects for the US, automation dreams, aeromodelling startups with the Airforce

My days were filled with achievements.
But my nights were filled with questions.

I became a professor in my hometown. Tied to a chair, staring into blank whiteboards, I realized —
"I was never built for sitting still. I was made to run, to fly, to burn."

The world called it success. I called it suffocation. Somewhere between the ticking clocks and fading dreams, I packed a bag and left.

Not to escape.
But to **find myself**.

And thus began my journey — In this part I am writing when I was wandering through hostel beds, across rivers and valleys, through Kasol's smoky nights and Goa's broken mornings — and finally back to Rishikesh.

Where, under the careless sky and misty mornings, destiny introduced me to *her*.
A girl who would unknowingly stitch herself into my story — the sweetest smile hiding the sharpest secrets — an intelligence officer, a RAW agent.

But at that time, on that first cold night, I knew nothing. I was just another restless traveller, stepping off a bus at Nepali Chowk, Rishikesh. The story was only beginning.

Chapter 1

Nepali Chowk, Rishikesh

The bus hissed to a stop, coughing out tired passengers into the heavy air of Rishikesh.
It was past midnight. Nepali Chowk buzzed with a strange, sleepless energy — food stalls throwing their last omelets on the pan, cab drivers lazily calling for customers, dogs weaving between tired feet.

He stepped down with a bag heavier than it looked and a heart lighter than it had been in years.

The night smelled of wet earth and adventure. He tightened the strap of his backpack, breathed in the smoky mist, and smiled without meaning to.There were no goodbyes left to send, no promises to keep.Only the road ahead — wild, open, unscripted.

Somewhere beyond the tangle of alleys and hostels, his story waited — hidden in laughter, in pain, in unexpected friendships, and in a girl whose eyes carried storms. But for now, he just walked, letting the city swallow him whole.

A hostel was waiting for him — cheap, creaky beds, and strangers who would become temporary families.
The first step had been taken.as he disappeared into the heartbeat of Rishikesh, the night quietly rewrote its stars.

The taxi driver, Bhim, tightened the last knot on the roof luggage before turning back with a smile.

It was decided — the taxi would be ours for the next three days.

Standing at Nepali Chowk, under the flickering tube lights and the busy hum of buses and travellers, he spotted familiar faces:

Rohit and Akash.

Old friends. Forgotten laughter.

Meeting Akash after five long years felt like flipping a dusty chapter in an old diary. The excitement was real — loud, rough hugs, wide smiles, unspoken stories.

Rafting and adventure talks had already started before they even left the parking area.

Dreams of the river currents, plans of mountains to climb.

They were alive again — and it felt different from the cities they had left behind.

They drove into Tapovan — a neighborhood stitched with hostels, cafés, and youth.

The streets buzzed with life: couples walking hand-in-hand, solo travellers sitting in clusters, guitars strumming from open balconies, and laughter riding the cold breeze.

The energy was contagious — like a town that had decided to never grow old.

Bhim parked the taxi carefully.

Backpacks slung over shoulders, they entered **GoStops Hostel** — a colorful building pulsing with music and conversations.

They checked into a shared dorm and quietly booked a private room as well — because in Tapovan, drinking in the open wasn't allowed, but memories needed their own space to ferment.

In the common area, he noticed her.
A girl with a magnetic aura — working intently on a laptop, her posture confident, her smile unforced.

She lent her laptop to a group of guys who requested it, without a flicker of hesitation.
Humble. Graceful. Unbothered by the chaos around her.

Moments later, they met another traveller — **Rahul**.
He was traveling with a girl named **Priya** — a soft-spoken woman working remotely for a multinational company.
Their relationship was difficult to read: somewhere between heartbreak and companionship.
Rahul carried the silent heaviness of a man who had lost more than he cared to admit, while Priya floated like someone trying to heal without saying it aloud.

It struck him how modern traveling had changed —
"**Destination work culture,**" he thought, observing Priya tapping away at her laptop while sipping hostel coffee. Workplaces had shrunk to backpacks; offices had been replaced by café tables.
Now the freedom had a new face.

The girl from the common area — the one with the gentle aura — recommended the hostel café's coffee.
There was something about her that stayed, even after she disappeared up the staircase.
Tired but buzzing with new beginnings, they decided to take showers, to breathe a little, to rest their road-weary bodies.

The journey had just begun, and on same scenario Tosh is writing the untold stories of Tapovan.

Outside, the streets of Rishikesh whispered promises of unscripted nights waiting just around the corner.

Inside, the hostel room was buzzing with life. The weather was pleasant, a soft chill in the air making every breath feel a little more alive. Everything was getting set for tomorrow — rafting and bungee were waiting for us, and our energy was already tuned toward the adventure.

Our stock was already full — Bombay Sapphire, Camino, premium whiskeys . The vibes were setting in slowly. We had decided earlier to first experience the incredible Ganga Aarti. All three of us — Akash, Rahul, and I — made our way through the buzzing streets towards Laxman Jhula. The evening Aarti at Sai Ghat was unforgettable, pulling not just devotees but youth too, who came to soak in the calm after the chaos.

On the way back, we stopped at a bakery near Sai Ghat — fresh cakes, still warm, filled the shop with sweet smells. The apple pie was heavenly — the kind of simple joy that stays with you longer than it should.

Returning to the hostel, we took a deep breath, ready for the night to unfold.

Near our room, Priya and her friend were already sitting outside, drinking openly in the common space, although it was actually against hostel rules. Our driver Bhimseth and one of our friends chose to crash early in the dorms, so they'd be fresh for rafting the next morning.

Meanwhile, inside our room, we started our own little party — slowly, unhurriedly. Akash went out first, getting called by Priya and others. After a moment, they called me too, and I joined in.

Introductions began over glasses. Priya was sipping Uttarakhand's local liquor, and her friend was gulping Old Monk — a classic choice for youngsters. The initial talks were casual — names, cities, what brought us here.

Frankly, I wasn't finding them interesting enough, so after a few polite exchanges, I returned to my room. I preferred silence over shallow conversations.

But the peace didn't last long. The hostel caretaker showed up soon, scolding Priya and the others — drinking in common spaces wasn't allowed. So, we did what travellers always do: adjusted. We opened our room to everyone, a little rebellion in the name of friendship.

Rahul and Priya came inside, joined by two more guys from nearby dorms. The discussions now felt livelier — memories of how hostels used to have wild, carefree vibes.

Outside, we could hear some dormitory guests complaining about hostel rules, they also want to enjoy in common area. But inside our small circle, introductions continued over laughter and clinking glasses.

After a few pegs, a girl passed by. She was Priya's friend, staying right beside her dorm.

Priya called out teasingly, "Hey, why don't you join us?"

She smiled, a little drunk already, her steps unsteady but her spirit shining through. As she walked in, the entire room seemed to brighten. There was something about her — something wildly free, yet heartbreakingly delicate.

Her hair was shoulder-length, perfectly messy in a way only careless freedom can achieve. She folded one leg over another casually and asked, "Aur bhai, ander hi baithe rahoge ya koi aur plan hai?"

Her voice — god, her voice — it wasn't just heard; it was felt. A slight vibration, a slight unsteadiness, but full of life. I wanted to keep listening to her, just like one listens to an old favorite song on loop.

She introduced herself casually. She was into export business, with a great sense of independence and personality. She mentioned she was working with an IB (Intelligence) background for the last few years, but didn't reveal much more about her role — just enough to spark curiosity.

And I — I was just observing.

Just watching.

I didn't want to miss a single moment.

We had already talked with Priya and Rahul about myself. They knew me — Nomad — the traveller who rarely shares personal details, who lives between destinations, between one unscripted night and another. Only my travel name was known to them, not my real story.

As I looked at her, everything else faded.

She mentioned casually, while sipping her drink, that she was adopted. That she often came to Rishikesh, especially around the death anniversary of her parents.

Then — without any shift in her brave smile — she said she had lost her fiancé just six months ago.

It hit me like a storm — yet she wore her smile so beautifully, so powerfully, that it almost made the pain invisible.

Almost.

Because when I looked carefully, beyond that bright laugh, beyond that shining charm, I could see it. The pain. Hidden deep behind her eyes.
Somehow, without even knowing her name fully, I felt it inside me — as if I had known her loss long before tonight.

Her freeness wasn't a rebellion; it was survival.
Her happiness wasn't a gift; it was a shield.

I whispered slowly to my friend, "She is mine. Nobody will flirt with her. Nobody will even look at her."

I was the unspoken boss of my small gang. And when I said something, it stayed.
So nobody even dared to.

But inside, it wasn't dominance. It was care. Fierce, protective care — the kind you feel when you see a wounded bird still trying to fly with broken wings.

Pain from the first moment. Pain so familiar, so deep, that it felt like meeting an old heartbreak in human form.

As conversations carried on, Priya watched me carefully. She whispered teasingly, "She's your type, you know. You both are nomads. She has that madness you love."

I laughed it off, brushing it aside lightly. "Dreams never come true, Priya," I said, pretending to be indifferent. "And she's way above me. High-class. I'm just a dusty nomad."

But my heart refused to listen to my head.

I didn't want to miss even a second of her presence. Every laugh, every sip, every glance was a silent poem.

She was texting someone constantly, looking at her phone, waiting for replies that maybe were never going to come.
After a while, she stepped outside to make a call.
I thought, Maybe she's already sent 1000 messages by now, smiling painfully at the thought.

Priya chuckled, watching her leave. She said, half-joking, half-serious, "Tosh, you should marry her. She's exactly your kind."

Inside, my heart agreed. Loudly.
But my lips said, "In one or two hours, Priya? How can anyone decide these things?"

I tried to act cool. To pretend I was unaffected. But inside, the battle was already lost.

She came back into the room, the same wild, shining spirit lighting up the space.
I locked my eyes on her again, unable to stop myself.

I know when I focus on someone with my full energy — my full kundalini — no one can escape. It's self-obsession, maybe. Or something deeper.

Her pain sat quietly behind her smiles.
I kept wondering: How can someone lose so much and still smile like this?

She spoke about her art — wall paintings in cafés around Rishikesh, with her friends.
Simple joys.
Lost worlds.

I watched her drink — 100 ml of liquor with just 10 ml of water — and not even a slight reaction on her face.
I wanted to correct her habits, protect her from herself.
I wasn't supposed to feel all this, but I was feeling it anyway.

She kept checking her phone. Kept expecting someone.
Someone who maybe wasn't answering her.
Just like her past, just like her lost promises, or just like she would to be her.

And me?

I just wanted to stay there. Watch her a little longer. Protect her without her asking. Carry her hidden sadness without words.

In the background, the party murmured on. Priya sighed about her own life — the struggles of being 34, the endless expectations, the silent wars fought alone.

And amidst all this, one unsaid thing was growing louder between us:

Two broken souls, recognizing each other's cracks.

Two Nomads, lost in a hostel room on a random night, in a town full of unanswered prayers.

The drinks were flowing, conversations were blending into the soft night, but my eyes were still locked on her. She was laughing with everyone, yet somewhere, I could feel she was hiding a thousand unsaid stories behind those smiles. Every small gesture of hers — adjusting her hair, sipping her drink, stealing glances at her phone — was speaking louder than words. I didn't know why, but it felt like if I didn't protect her tonight, a part of me would regret it forever. Priya and others kept laughing and talking, but in my mind, only her presence echoed.

I was listening to her deeply. She asked what was my plan for the next day.
I told her about our rafting plan, and then she suggested we could also visit Tehri.

Excited by the idea, I called my batchmate, an engineer at the Tehri Dam, and told him I was coming with friends. I requested VIP entry to the turbines and inside sections. He agreed and asked for our ID cards to make the passes.
It felt like everything was falling into place — a new plan, a new adventure.

Still, my eyes were stuck on her.
While talking, she was rubbing her legs against mine — her touch was appealing, magnetic.

I understood something was connecting here, something unsaid.

Suddenly, she got a call.
She stepped outside, talking lovingly and deeply with someone. I stayed inside, just silently observing her from afar. Honestly, I didn't care whom she was talking to — my mind was firm, when I like someone, I like them, and that's it.

Inside my head, a storm was raging: Was she the one I was unknowingly searching for all this time?
Somewhere deep inside, the questions melted into a silent sweet "maybe."

After finishing her call, she came back, gave us all a sweet goodbye, and promised she'd join the Tehri trip tomorrow. She left our small party with a softness that stayed floating in the air even after she had gone.

As soon as she left, Priya immediately asked me —
"So, do you like her or not?"

I was shocked.
Why is everyone noticing?
I tried to change the topic. It was too early. I didn't even know her properly — and, of course, there's always a silent male ego hiding behind casual conversations.

Before leaving, she had casually shared her number with me — officially, for some "Jaipur property work."
But I knew it was much more than just business.

The party drifted again — now only Rahul, Priya, Akash, and me remained.

Everyone was drunk. Cigarettes were finished. Rahul decided to crash into his dorm bunk.

Now it was just three of us.
My mind was stuck somewhere — actually not "somewhere," but in her.

Suddenly Priya, full of energy, pulled out some weed.
She took a puff and passed it to me and Akash.
Though I usually avoid these things, that night was different — intoxicated already by her thoughts, I accepted.

I started singing.
Even though I knew I was terrible at it, I sang — for her.

Priya said,
"You're a good singer. You should sing for her someday."

Even I smiled. Maybe she was right — not about my voice, but about the feeling behind it.

We began a random Truth and Dare game — like every hostel story that goes crazy at night.

The conversation slowly slipped towards bold, cheeky, and then erotic sides.
Akash couldn't handle the intoxication anymore — he fell asleep backward on the floor, leaving just two players now: Me and Priya.

Priya offered me another puff.
The night had completely wrapped me now.
Under the hazy sky of hostel lights, she asked with her mischievous smile —

"Tell me your real name, your number, or at least your Insta ID?"

I smiled, locked my half-drunk eyes into hers, and whispered:
"Destiny ne chaha, toh agli baar zarur bataunga."

She loved that reply.
Priya leaned closer, playful yet serious.

And then, without any more words,she asked i would like to do one thing if you allow. she did something unexpected —
She suddenly kissed me.
Firmly, warmly — on my lips, for almost two minutes.

Then she set back, breathing heavily, her eyes a little guilty.
She softly said,
"I'm so sorry..."

Chapter 2

After the Kiss — The Last Raft and The Unfinished Goodbye

After that long, energetic, almost breathless kiss, she leaned back into her chair, her eyes flickering between apology and unspoken desire.

I sat there, intoxicated — not just by whiskey and weed, but by the rawness of the moment.

Yet, deep inside, I was still the same man — the one who never believed in love, who had spent years counselling friends:

"Don't fall in love, it's meaningless."

That was my truth. Emotions were toys I never wanted to play with.

Two minutes passed in silence, her breath slowly settling.

Then she looked at me with that same mischievous glint and said softly,

"I want one more…"

Without waiting for permission, she leaned in again — lips crashing onto mine with more hunger, more abandon.

When it ended, she smiled lightly and asked,

"Can you please tell me your name? Or give me some ID where I can text you when I travel next? I won't bother you… just text."

I stayed true to myself — arrogance blended with mystery — and replied,

"Destiny ne chaha, aur agli baar mile, to zarur bataunga."

Even though she was from Mangalore and didn't know Hindi well, she understood every weight of that sentence.

Her charm didn't fade.

She smiled deeper and slowly tried to slide back onto the bed — where my friend lay fast asleep like an infant.

I resisted.

But there are limits to resistance when someone holds you tightly, her touch exploring, her breath quickening again, i slept infantly.

It was 8 AM by then — the door was ajar, no latch, daylight pouring in, and no lights off.

Suddenly, my other friend barged in and casually asked,

"Should we get ready for rafting?"

A few minutes later, he returned and jokingly splashed a jug of water on me.

That broke everything.

The intoxication, the fog in my mind — all gone.

I sat up instantly, gathered myself, and asked her to leave politely.

I thanked whatever higher force existed that things didn't cross the line completely.

The morning after that long, charged night, she left gently, with a soft smile that carried neither regret nor expectation.

I felt unexpectedly light — as though something heavy had been lifted off me.

my mind was clear.

I took an hour of sleep and by the time I woke up, our plan for rafting had already begun to take shape.

Akash woke up too — but beyond my guidance or intention, he drifted towards their dorm.

I later found out he was chatting with Priya and Veda, casually asking them for their IDs for the Tehri Dam visit we had planned.

But his intentions weren't as clean as they appeared.

When Veda (Anku) handed him her phone to send her ID, he sneakily saved his number in her contact list under a flirty name like "Babes" or "Loving One".

It was typical playful flirting — something I never wanted to involve myself in.

I was still lost in thoughts of Veda and was stuck there, caught somewhere between admiration and detachment.

It pained me somewhere deep — but I didn't regret anything.

Veda had already exchanged numbers with me the night before, but not social media — just basic contact.

Akash, noticing that she shared her WhatsApp number with him but hadn't given me the same, began to think he was ahead in the "game."

He assumed she didn't even notice me.

But I knew better.

Connections made from purity cannot be tampered with — and I was pure from inside, with no bad intentions towards anyone.

Soon after, Akash approached Priya again — she was sitting in the first-floor common area with a coffee.

Another friend later told me Akash was casually touching Priya's cheeks, enjoying light flirtation.

I stayed away from all this.

I'd seen enough.

We left for rafting and enjoyed it immensely — water splashing, laughter echoing through the valley.

Later, we began talking again about our Tehri plan.

Akash called Veda to invite her — she said she'd come in a few minutes as she was busy painting at somewhere near Sai Ghat.

Many conversations happened that day, but she never showed up And to be honest — I didn't want to go to Tehri without her. Without her presence, the place didn't call to me.

We dropped the plan.

Akash kept calling her to join us at the party that night.

She never said no directly — but she didn't come back either.

I kept telling Akash to call her again.

Deep down, I just wanted to see her once more.

But by observing their dynamic, I had quietly accepted that she would remain a sweet dream for me — nothing more.

I didn't want to step between them or complicate things.

I stayed in my zone.

But after the whirlwind of the last night, and seeing how people were interacting, I didn't feel like meeting anyone again.

I had no desire to indulge in hash or more games.

I withdrew into myself.

That night, many groups from across India arrived at the hostel.

I declared that only boys would be allowed in my drinks circle — and strangely, it felt like I was Ram among Vanars.

Many boys gravitated towards me, respecting me, saying "Bhaiya, aap boliye kya karna hai, aapka aadesh chahiye."

Nobody sat at the same level as me that night — I felt elevated in my solitude.

Akash, meanwhile, enjoyed himself with a new group of girls from another batch.

Priya, as told to me later, went to some other guy's room and enjoyed herself there too.

I didn't care.

I wandered the streets of Rishikesh with my group of boys — at one point, we even went to Sai Ghat hoping to catch a glimpse of Veda (since she'd said earlier she was there).

She wasn't there.

We returned empty-handed.

The next morning, as we prepared to leave, I finally saw her again — tired, dehydrated, but still calm.

She met her friend Shivani near the hostel gate, sipping water from a bottle like a child.

Watching her like that, so tender and simple, felt oddly relaxing.

We exchanged brief goodbyes.

I never asked for her contact — I always stuck to my sense of masculinity and boundaries.

We left the hostel soon after.

But as fate would have it — soon after departure, I received a WhatsApp message from her:

"Hi."

That single message made me smile deeply.

All my friends left Rishikesh, but I stayed one extra day as always — I had a habit of spending an extra day to simply sleep and soak in the place.

I booked another hostel, texted her again, but our timings didn't match.

I left Rishikesh the next day — with a heart full of cozy memories and no desire to return too soon.

Chapter 3

The Call That Shook Me

Exactly one year had passed.
I was back at the same hostel, on the same bed, in the same silent corner of Rishikesh where so many unscripted memories were born.
I had returned here not just as a traveller — but as a writer.
My fingers were eager to bring back every faded heartbeat and forgotten glance onto the pages.
I was so excited to write. So ready to pour everything out.

But then — my phone vibrated.
A call.

It was her.
Veda .

Her voice came soft, steady, and final.

"I am going to get married in a few days," she said.

That one sentence pierced deeper than I expected.
My hands froze over the keyboard.
My breathing stumbled.
My palms began to sweat and shake.
It felt like time had folded onto itself, and all those moments — her smile, our talks, the silent understandings — came crashing down into a single painful blur.

The same bed, the same room, the same air — everything that once gave me peace now felt suffocating.
I didn't know where to look, what to feel, or why to even sit there anymore.

I was shaking.
My body was here — but my mind had drowned somewhere else.
The beautiful nights of last year had turned into heavy, frightening shadows today.
I didn't want to stay.
I didn't want to write anymore.
I didn't even know how to hold myself together on that chair.

I closed my eyes and leaned back, hoping the silent Rishikesh air would calm me down.
But inside, I knew…
Something had ended.
Something that maybe never even began properly.

I stayed silent.
I didn't reply to her much.
I didn't tell anyone what just happened.

I just sat there, alone — letting that hostel night wrap itself around me once again,
but this time… not with excitement,
but with a quiet, unbearable ache.

I didn't cry. I didn't even move. I just sat there—completely blank.

I wasn't angry. I wasn't even surprised.
I was… rewinding.

Three, maybe few years of my life began to replay behind my eyes. Not in the usual way people say *"life flashed before my eyes"*, but like I was scrubbing through old memories on a dusty videotape.

Hostels. Railway platforms. Sleepless nights with clap box and the sound of waves.
A revolving door of faces I never remembered, and moments I never forgot.

I was the **Unethical Traveller**—not unethical by my acts, but by my emotions.
I entered people's lives quietly, deeply, and left without warning. I made connections, but never commitments.
I shared stories, but never hearts.
I touched souls, but never called anyone *home*.

And now, the only person who ever made me think about *staying*—was calling me to tell me *she was leaving*.
That night, I didn't sleep. I lay on the bed, motionless, as Goa began to rise in my mind.

Chapter 4

The Playground of moments – Goa

Before I take you to those golden shores of Goa, let me tell you something honestly — something about the person I used to be.

I had lived many lives before Goa.
Nights full of hostel stories, countless cups of tea with strangers, wild parties, drunken confessions, endless laughter, and beds shared not with love — but with fleeting moments and raw conversations.

I wasn't the kind of man searching for love.
No.
I never believed in it.
In fact, I often counselled others to stay away from love.
I would say —
"Don't fall into it. It complicates everything. It weakens you. Stay free. Stay light."

And I lived exactly like that.

I was emotionless but clean from inside.
Yes — my heart was untouched by love, but it was untouched by hatred or bad intentions too.

I simply floated through life —
grabbing stories, collecting moments, leaving before attachments grew roots.

From Kasol to Rishikesh, from desert sands to high mountains —
I had built a world of fun, freedom, and unscripted memories.
Hostel confessions, river rafting plans, silent hikes, shared smokes, unknown kisses — all of it filled my diary.

I was happy.
Truly.
Or so I thought.
And then…
I went to Goa.
Goa —
Where the waves didn't just crash on the shores —
They crashed straight into my carefully built walls.

Because in Goa, I met Greta.
A girl from Germany.
A story that wasn't like any of the unscripted hostel nights I had lived before.

In fact, I proudly carried my rulebook:
"No love. No attachments. No weakness. Just collect stories and move on."

It all began…
on those sands,
under that foreign sky,
with her smile.

For now,
Let me take you back to Goa,
where lust, freedom, unscripted beds and unchained moments wrote their wildest chapters in my diary.

Chapter 5

Goa — My Playground of Freedom

Goa is not just a place on the map.
It's an emotion.
A pilgrimage — especially for engineers like us who wait the whole year to escape, breathe free, and feel alive.

Lacs of people visit Goa every year. I have been visiting for many years now.
I have seen Goa not as a tourist but as a old school friend growing together —
watching its every lane, beach, and colony shift colors like a slow, unfolding story.

I have seen Baga Beach change in front of my eyes.
There was a time when Baga was carefree — the sand soft underfoot, shacks echoing with live music, and strangers turning into friends over seafood and beer.
But gradually, I witnessed fights breaking out, small-time robberies scaring visitors, and the soul of Baga getting clouded.
It hurt to see it.
I walked through the empty stretches of Anjuna and Vagator, once so peaceful that you could hear your thoughts blend with the sound of waves.
Now those same beaches pulse with neon lights, loud music, crowded shacks, and a nightlife that rarely sleeps.

I remember Arambol too —
once a pocket of foreign artists and peaceful seekers, where people did yoga at sunrise and played handpans on the sand.

I saw it convert into darker nights — tangled in sex scandals, secret rooms, and lost faces searching for temporary highs.

I have wandered the narrow lanes of the Russian colony in Morjim.
I saw peaceful Russian families build a life near the beach, quiet and distant from tourist chaos.
Over the years, whispers spread — of the Russian mafia stepping in, changing the undercurrent of that calm space.
But I kept walking — observing, not judging.

And yet…
Despite all this evolution,
Goa never loses its essence.

It still breathes freedom.
It still lets you rediscover yourself every time you arrive.
It doesn't matter how many times you visit —
there is always something new,
something that pulls you deeper into its story.

I remember trekking through the forests around Querim Beach —
a place so raw and untouched that for a moment, I forgot I was in Goa.
It's now slowly developing, but still, it holds that charm of discovery that most won't find on Google Maps.

Whenever someone Googles "Places to visit in Goa,"
they see Baga and Calangute at the top of the list.
But I don't go there anymore.
I haven't for many years.
The crowd is bad, the noise endless, and the charm diluted.

I chase the Goa that breathes —
not the one that shouts.

Every year around the Sunburn Festival, Goa transforms
entirely.
It becomes a 24-hour living, breathing festival.
Private parties run for 48 hours straight —
no breaks, no sleep, just music, lights, and people surrendering
to the moment.

That's why Goa is precious to me.
Here, nobody knows you.
You can live exactly the way you want.
You don't carry your identity here — you carry your curiosity.
And that is enough.

For the Sunburn of that year,
I planned my trip with Pandit, my old travel companion.
We are not the kind of travellers who move in large groups.
We like it simple — two people or solo —
enough to blend into the crowd yet remain untouched by it.

There is always an excitement in every person to go global
— especially in this time of globalisation. In the long
journey of discovering a partner or exploring oneself, every
individual carries somewhere inside them a silent desire to
make a globalized choice.
I have seen this craze clearly — among foreign tourists
in India desperate to explore Indian connections, and
equally among Indians curious and excited to discover
foreigners.

I remember meeting an Italian friend once in Goa. He was
desperately looking for an Indian girlfriend — as if his visit

to Goa would not be complete without that connection. On the other side, I saw an Indian sportswoman who was eagerly, almost restlessly, searching for a foreign boyfriend, maybe for fun, maybe for experience, maybe for stories to tell.
It happens both ways.

I have also seen another side of Goa. Many people — robbed of ethics and driven by cheap mentalities — land in Goa with wrong intentions. They don't come with the purity of travel or friendship. They come to exploit, and in the end, they themselves are robbed, either of their belongings or their experiences.
But I say — if you go to Goa with a pure soul, with a friendly heart and an open mind, Goa will return to you each and every experience far beyond your expectation. It rewards the genuine traveller.

We landed in Goa on 27th December.
The winter sun was crisp,
Ready to write new stories,
Ready to collect new moments.
We landed at Dabolim Airport, Goa.
The winter sun felt different — crisp, bright, and familiar.
This time, like always, our destination was already decided: North Goa.
We were here for Sunburn Festival, and the plan was fixed well in advance.

We landed at Dabolim Airport, Goa.
The winter sun felt different — crisp, bright, and familiar.
This time, like always, our destination was already decided: North Goa.
We were here for Sunburn Festival, and the plan was fixed well in advance.

But the airport was far from where the real energy lived.
Arambol — our chosen base — was on the other end of Goa, almost kissing the northern edge.
Known for its foreigner-friendly atmosphere and offbeat vibe, Arambol had always attracted a different kind of traveller — raw, real, slightly reckless.

Due to the Sunburn rush, all bunk beds were already booked across most hostels.
So we had arranged to stay in tents at a local hostel near Arambol beach — a kind of setup that blended perfectly with Goa's free-spirited energy.

From the airport, we planned to hire a taxi to Arambol, but in Goa, things often fall into place naturally.

In the friendlier air of Goa, where strangers become companions in minutes, we found two girls from Indore looking to pool a ride in the same direction.
They asked politely if they could join us, and we agreed.
Why not?
This is Goa — every journey is a chance to make new stories.
And so the ride began —
Four strangers in a cab, chasing music, plans, and promises of nights that didn't end on clocks.

We all spoke freely, like people do when they know this isn't forever.
The ride toward North Goa was smooth — beaches flashing past windows, the vibe slowly building with every kilometre.

That night, we had already planned to go clubbing, to shake off the travel fatigue and sync with Goa's rhythm.
From the next day, Sunburn would begin, and the energy would multiply.
We knew what was coming —
music, madness, and maybe something more.
As the taxi rolled out from Dabolim Airport, the conversation sparked almost immediately.

Pandit and I, both **Mechanical Engineers**, introduced ourselves casually.
To our surprise, the girls from Indore — both working in an IT company — opened up quickly.
The air in the car became lighter, more relaxed.
Maybe it was the Goa vibe.
Maybe it was the fact that everyone in that cab was **somewhere between structured life and wild detours.**

They told us someone was already waiting for them at their booked place — but as the conversation deepened, that urgency slowly disappeared.
They laughed at our stories, listened closely when we spoke about life and choices.
They said it felt safe with us.
Maybe they were just being kind.
Or maybe, in a place like Goa, **clarity comes faster when you're far from your usual world.**

We shared our plans — **Sunburn tomorrow, LPK club tonight**.
Pandit casually invited them to join us at LPK.
They paused, whispered to someone on call, then smiled.

"We're skipping our old plan. We'll come with you."

They changed their destination — choosing to come with us to our **tent hostel in Arambol**.
The sun was dipping low as we reached.
And the moment we entered the hostel compound, **something felt right**.

There was an **open bar**, fairy lights hanging from trees, low music playing, and people sitting in circles — all under the soft, golden glow of Goa's evening.
The hostel was **run by foreign volunteers from Workaway** — and their free spirit reflected in the way the place moved.
Even the girls were impressed.
"Feels like a movie set," one of them said, smiling.

We freshened up, changed, and **rented a car for the night**.

By now, the mood was set.
They asked us if they could invite some of their friends.
We nodded — no Goa plan is ever complete without last-minute additions.
They made a few calls.
Their group joined at the venue, but **hesitated at the gate —** surprised by the **stag entry fee, even for girls**.

We stepped in to help — offered a couple of couple entries, paid for a bit — but then drew the line.
We weren't going to cover everyone's party.

The energy shifted.
Pandit's conversation with one of the girls got intense.
No shouting — just sharp silence.
He nodded once, turned around, and **walked off with his partner** toward a nearby hotel.

Now it was just me and **Aarti** — one of the Indore girls.
We stayed at the club for a while longer, then decided to leave.

But Pandit had taken the car.
So we did the Goa thing:
Hitchhiking.

At 4:00 a.m., we stood under a dim streetlight, trying to get a ride.
Music still echoed from a distance. The world was slow.
We tried for almost an hour. Nothing.

And then — a car stopped.
A **gentleman named Arun**, soft-spoken and warm, offered us a ride.
He wasn't just passing by — he was **the owner of an old-school local hostel near Anjuna,** a place called *Wonderful Goan.*
Simple, authentic, and full of true Goan charm.

On the ride, I promised him —
"I'll stay at your place tomorrow, after Sunburn."

The next morning, Aarti woke up early.
She smiled and walked over to where I was still half-asleep on the mattress in the tent.
Without a word, she hugged me — tight and warm — and whispered a heartfelt "Thank you" for the last night.
The hitchhiking, the club, the whole experience.
"This will stay with me for long," she said.
She asked softly, "We'll stay in touch, right? Forever?"

I smiled.

Not because I believed in forever —
But because sometimes, moments like these don't need answers.

I told them I'd be leaving now — heading to a different place for new vibes.
That part of the story — the morning goodbye — was actually Pandit's to own.
He had his own closure to find.

I left the hostel, packed light, and moved to Bunkd Hostel in Anjuna — a place I had already decided to stay for the coming days.
Fresh energy, new crowd, no expectations.
I didn't even save numbers.
I just texted Pandit my new location and told him I'd be heading straight to Sunburn.

The energy at Sunburn was insane.
Drinks, dance, music, madness.
The sea of people, the endless beats, the hypnotic lights — it all blurred into one unforgettable storm of life.
I was floating through it.

Sometime in the afternoon, I got a message — Pandit was on his way to meet me there.
But before I could find him, I spotted something strange near one of the entry gates.

There he was — Pandit, standing beside one of the Indore girls, and she was crying.
Beside them stood a Deputy Superintendent of Police (DSP) in full uniform.
My heart sank.
The DSP looked serious.

And to my shock — Pandit pointed directly at me.
I froze.
What had he done?
Was it a scene? A complaint? A misunderstanding?
My mind raced.
Should I walk away quietly?
Should I prepare for bail, just in case?
But before I could decide, a couple of policemen approached
me —
not aggressively, but with unexpected respect.

"Sir, DSP sahib is calling you. He's inviting you for a VIP
entry."

Wait. What?

I walked up slowly.

The DSP came forward, extended his hand and smiled.
"Hello, SDM Sir."

I was stunned for a moment, but I nodded back smoothly.
"Hello, DSP."

Pandit just gave me a mischievous smile.
Now the whole picture was clear —
He had used his Gazetted Officer ID to pull this stunt. since
I was one too, he played it perfectly.

The DSP gave us both a nod of respect and handed us his
contact number,
saying, "If there's ever any trouble — police or otherwise —
just call me directly."

Policemen around us saluted, and suddenly we were no longer just two guys in a crowd —
We were two names that mattered.

We entered VIP like legends.

Inside Arena Five, the lights got brighter, the music louder, and the pegs stronger.
But before anything else, I turned to Pandit —and slapped him, hard and fast.
Not out of anger —
but out of shock, laughter, and pure old-school friendship.
"You idiot! You should've informed me before you changed my post over a drink!"

He laughed.
"Come on, bro. It's not new for us. In a world where everyone's struggling for their identity — we just borrowed a few stripes to make it through."

We laughed — all three of us.
Me, Pandit, and the girl.

We clinked our glasses, no guilt, no ego — just pure unscripted madness.
And just like that, the Sunburn story had already become one of those forever stories.
After that wild VIP entry twist, everything else just flowed.

Music. Dance. Strangers. Madness.
We melted into the crowd — the kind of crowd where nobody asks your name, and nobody cares where you're from.

In college life, we're often stuck in formals, routines, same old shades of clothing and behavior.
Even though I was never fully that type — I still lived mostly in sober colours, cargo pants, and a quiet face.

But here?
Here we were different.
Dressed in **pop-up colours, open shirts, funky glasses —** we weren't just attending Sunburn, we were **living it.**
Drinks poured freely. Beats hit harder.
The world around us spun with no rules, and for once, we didn't care.

We danced.
We shouted.
We clapped with strangers and vibed like we'd known each other for years.

By the time the music faded and the lights dimmed, the **Sunburn night had carved itself into us forever**.

We said our goodbyes to that Indore girl.
There was no emotional drama. No promises.
Just a smile, a hug, and a shared knowing — that whatever happened, it was one hell of a night.

Pandit and I headed back to **Bunkd Hostel in Anjuna**.
Back to the base.
Back to where **the next chapter** was waiting quietly to begin.

Chapter 6

Nomad and Pandit Arrive with Smoking Meditation

Goa has a strange way of blurring time. Sunburn might have ended at 10 PM, but for us, the night was just starting to breathe.

We landed at **Bunkd Hostel, Anjuna**—dusty, dazed, and dripping with the last notes of the festival. The hostel walls pulsed with energy, strung with fairy lights and scrawled notes from Nomads before us. But what caught our eye was something unexpected—**a handwritten message on the party board:**

"Welcome to the Party Night, Nomad and Pandit."

That was us.

Even in our half-exhausted state, it sparked something. We'd only come to crash on our beds. Our bodies ached for rest. But the walls whispered otherwise.

Music thumped from a small Bluetooth speaker in the garden. Laughter rose like smoke. The air had that warm, free scent of whiskey and dust. We paused at our dorms for a moment, checked our beds, then looked at each other. Something inside both of us stirred. This wasn't just a party—it was a different kind of world.

We walked back out.

And in that moment, both of us knew it—this was the kind of space we'd always dreamed of. **Far from our so-called "high-value society"** where class and caution ruled the day. This was raw, real. A place that could survive on bare minimum things—**and premium whiskey.**

We wandered into the garden area, where people from every corner of the world mingled like childhood friends. Volunteers from **Walkaway** and other travel networks floated around effortlessly—cleaning floors, greeting guests, pouring drinks—all without any manager, time card, or orders barked. The entire hostel ran on shared effort, silent respect, and pure flow. Foreigners were doing everything—**from reception work to running the party.** Not for salary. Just for the story.

I stepped aside for a smoke and some quiet, and that's when I met **Varun**, one of the owners, and **Paul**, his long-time friend and hostel mate. Paul was laidback, with a soft accent and sharp eyes. His Goan girlfriend, **Ramaya**, joined us—curious, grounded, and glowing with beach-town calm.

We shook hands, exchanged casual hellos, and within minutes, we found ourselves deep in conversation. I told them about our interest in opening a space like this. One that pulses with energy, welcomes Nomads, and lives on its own rules. Aarti—Pandit—chimed in too. It didn't take long for the vibe to click.

Paul and Ramaya leaned in. You could feel their interest wasn't forced. They saw something in us. Some madness. Some potential. And they affirmed it:

"You should do it. The world needs more places like this."

They introduced us to their volunteers—each with their own wild backstory, some on sabbatical, others just lost in the most beautiful way.

We stood there, feeling like we'd slipped into the right place at the right time. That's when **Sui Chain** walked up.

"Hi," she said, casually. Like we already knew her.

She was from **Singapore,** and one glance told you she wasn't your average traveller. Her story flowed out—**riding across the world on her own bike,** collecting dust and dreams from every continent. There was a fire in her voice, but peace in her eyes. The kind of balance only found in people who've seen both chaos and clarity.

We were instantly drawn to her—not just because she was unique, but because she reminded us of why we were there.

This wasn't a vacation.

It was a calling.

The night was slipping deeper, like the silence between tracks at a good party. Aarti had already vanished into her world somewhere inside the hostel, probably lost in laughter, chai, or a stranger's story. Pandit, mellow and toasted by now, raised his bottle toward me and chuckled:

""Guru," he said, "this world needs your madness."

I smiled. The name stuck harder than I expected.

We were still in the courtyard where we had been speaking with Varun, Paul, and Ramaya. Conversations were flowing like unfiltered rum—raw, unexpected, and warm in the chest. People came and went, asking us about our travels, about India, about opening our own space someday. There was something magnetic about the moment—like we had earned a strange respect in a place we had only just arrived at.

Then Sui Chain returned.

She was different now—curious, more open, her posture relaxed but eyes still searching. She sat back with us again. Ramaya had gone inside to grab a jacket, Paul was talking to a guest, and suddenly it was just Sui, Pandit, and me.

That's when she began to speak—really speak.

She shared her journey without dressing it up. Before India, she was riding through Pakistan on her motorbike—alone. Faced tough roads, security checks, even fear. But nothing had shaken her like the invisible unrest she carried inside.

"India feels safer, but I don't feel centred. I feel… disturbed. Not by a place, but by something inside me."

She pulled on her cigarette like it held all the questions she didn't have words for.

"I don't earn much. I work random jobs for a few months, save up, and then ride again. That's how I've come this far. But now, my visa is about to expire. I leave tomorrow."

Her words didn't need drama. They carried a raw kind of truth—like sand carried in the cuffs of a traveller's jeans.

I listened without interrupting. And then, as if the night knew exactly when to shift gears, the conversation drifted to meditation.

She said she had tried it before—at an ashram somewhere, under a Bodhi tree, with robed men chanting—but it never really connected.

That's when I stepped in. Not from ego, not to teach—but because something inside me knew it was time to share.

"You don't need robes or Sanskrit chants. You don't need to sit under the perfect banyan tree. Meditation isn't about posing—it's about peeling off everything you're not."

She looked at me, intrigued but cautious.

"You're smoking," I said, gently. "Let's begin there. Let's do smoking meditation."

A few people nearby raised eyebrows. Someone whispered, someone laughed. But Sui? She nodded, slowly. She was ready.

I guided her—not to silence the world, but to hear herself inside the noise.

"Feel the cigarette," I said softly. "The weight in your hand. The heat of the fire. The draw of the smoke. burn it consciously, see it, observe your things, what you are going to do. Don't rush. Just… observe and be calm, don't fight with your thoughts and let them come inside, don't try to stop them"

She followed. The courtyard shifted. Conversations quieted. Even Pandit went still.

Fifteen minutes passed in a different time zone. No app. No timer. Just two people meditating with burning tobacco and burning questions.

When we opened our eyes, she exhaled like she hadn't in years.

"That… that was something else," she whispered. "I've travelled across countries… and in just a few minutes… I feel like I've finally landed."

She stood up slowly, stepped back, folded her hands with a warm smile and said:

"Guruji… namaste."

And with that, it was done, she shared some goodies with gesture to me and given a Russian currency as it was her travel memory, she shared with me and talks goes on.

The courtyard buzzed again, but differently. The whispers were new now. Some were impressed, some confused, some a little jealous. But no one could deny they had just witnessed something real.

Sui hugged me before leaving. No drama, just a sincere gesture.

"Next time," she said, "I'll ride to your hometown. I'll bring 10–11 bikers with me. You'll teach us this kind of meditation again?"

I laughed.

"I'll host you. Don't worry. You're most welcome."

And with that, she disappeared into the night like a firefly that had shown just enough light.

In Bunkd Hostel, every morning begins with yoga or breathwork sessions by volunteers. Every night ends with music, madness, and moments like this. But that night, something shifted. I didn't become anyone famous. I didn't sell anything.

But in a corner of Goa, I became a meditation master without trying—because I didn't teach a method. I just shared a moment.

And sometimes, that's all it takes.

The night refused to end. Just when you thought the energy had peaked, it evolved into something else.

More people kept joining our circle in the courtyard. First came **Ronaldo from Bangalore**, his vibe chilled, urban, the kind of guy who blended easily with everyone. Then a **guy from Haryana**, with a rugged Haryanvi accent. Not long after, a known face in the hostel showed up—a lanky, spaced-out man everyone referred to as the **"Smoke-Up Baba."**

The group swelled to seven, maybe eight of us.

And among them was a **19-year-old kid**—wild-eyed, restless, glowing with artificial energy. He hadn't slept in three days. Said he had done **LSD, smoke-up, weed, tabs**—

everything. He offered it casually, like candy at a birthday party.

That moment reminded me: no matter how free this place was, you had to walk with your **own standard**. With your own **mindset**. This was paradise, yes—but also a testing ground. You could get high on energy or lost in the haze. The choice was yours. I smiled politely, declined, and watched the night unfold without giving in.

Then, someone sparked it.

Shayari session began.

People settled down. Cushions were dragged out. A few beers were cracked open. Paul **and his girlfriend** joined the circle—he had a scruffy charm, she had that calm presence, and together they brought some grounding energy to the chaos.

Someone started with a few lines in English, someone added Hindi. And I? I waited for the silence between verses.

Then I said it, **in full flow**, without a pause:

"Beeti thi zindagi doston ke sang,
Doston ke sang bita tha zamana,
Meri bas ek aakhiri khwahish hai,
Mujhe mere college mein dafnana…
Mujhe mere college mein dafnana."

The words hung in the air. Silence. Then soft claps. Then whistles. It wasn't just applause—it was resonance. People felt it. You could see it in their eyes, those who'd lived a life of hostels and heartbreaks, who had loved and lost in classrooms.

The mood turned poetic.

That's when I noticed it: an old **clap box** leaning on the side near the wall. Behind it was a **Shiva painting**, hand-drawn, with wild brush strokes and soulful depth. Around it was scattered **classical and modern instruments**—a broken ukulele, a half-tuned guitar, and a dusty djembe.

The speaker nearby was junk. But vibes? **Vibes were gold.**

I picked up the clapbox and started tapping along to old Indian Bollywood classics. No practice, no perfection—just feel. Someone started singing an old Kishore song and just like that, music became our language. We played like children who'd just discovered rhythm.

We didn't care about disturbing anyone—but yes, we probably were. Some rooms had their lights off, and we were unintentionally waking dreamers. But who cared? We were dreamers too—**louder ones.**

After a while, **Paul and Ramaya left**—with that satisfied tiredness of people who had lived a full evening. A few goodbyes, a couple of hugs.

And then, someone said it.

"Let's go for a walk… to **Darling Bar Street**."

It was already past midnight, maybe close to 2. But in Goa, time is as flexible as your heartbeat. So we walked out—

barefoot or in slippers—toward that neon glow of **Darling Bar,** a street full of chaos, cheap drinks, loud music, shady promises, and unexpected magic.

The real journey of the night had only just begun.

Chapter 7

"Darling Bar Diaries: The Flame Named Diya"

The walk to Darling Bar Street wasn't new to us. But something about that night hit differently. Maybe it was the whiskey, maybe the company, or maybe the chaos we'd all carried with us silently for too long. Either way, something was about to unfold.

Darling Bar used to be one of those classic Goan joints. Before COVID, it was a heartbeat for foreigners — wild dance floors, open beach parties, neon paint and bare feet moving to house music until the sky changed color. But now? The energy was split. The crowd had become a mix — more Indian, more urban, fewer hippies, but the soul of the place still clung to its Portuguese walls.

I was already too far gone. The kind of drunk where memories become puzzle pieces. What I remember clearly is the vibe — warm yellow bulbs swinging slightly in the breeze, music bleeding from a cracked speaker, and strangers dancing like it was their last night on earth. Everything else? A blur I rebuilt from photos and friends' retellings.

As soon as we arrived, one of our boys tripped and fell trying to rush into the bar. That single moment pulled in a group of strangers who came forward to help him up. We didn't notice much — everyone was laughing, moving, buzzing. Pandit and a few others got stuck at a nearby bakery stall, captivated by a gorgeous girl serving pastries with a grin that could disarm a soldier. They tried their best, throwing clumsy charm at her while stuffing their faces with croissants.

Meanwhile, I drifted — alone, detached, weightless.

That's when I found myself in a new circle. A mix of couples and solo Nomads. Among them was her. A girl named Diya — or at least, that's what they told me. From South Delhi, classy, magnetic, and so stunning that I genuinely felt she wasn't real. she was so beautiful.

I started talking to her — casually at first. Then bolder. Something clicked. She smiled, leaned in, and accepted the drink I offered. The boyfriend beside her noticed but didn't say much initially. Until I made it obvious. I told her clearly:

"I'm here only for your company."

It was wild. Bold. Reckless. But it was honest.

To handle the situation, I quickly called Pandit and whispered the plan. He pulled her boyfriend aside, handed him drink after drink until the guy was completely sloshed, then took him to the washroom, locked the door, and returned with that satisfied smirk on his face.

I walked away with Diya. Just the two of us, walking slowly toward the quiet Mandovi road nearby. The breeze was gentle, almost cinematic. Our voices grew softer. Somewhere between laughter and silence, we kissed.

We kept walking, hand in hand. My memory fails after that, but the photo I saw in the morning was clear — I was lying in her lap, under a streetlight, with her fingers running through my hair. I had no idea how long we sat there or what else happened.

She gave me her ID, her number, something. I don't even know what name I saved it under. Might've been a fake name. Might've been a real one lost in my phone's chaos.

But then — drama returned.

Pandit came running, shouting breathlessly:

"Bhago b""d, lafda ho gaya!""

Her boyfriend had broken loose, somehow escaped the washroom, and was raging. The bakery girl had also joined in. A verbal fight started erupting. Our crew, as always, stayed cool. No punches, no pushing — just damage control.

Pandit was holding them off, creating distance so I could leave safely. That's our rule — don't mess up the energy of a place. No ego battles. No scenes. We respect where we go. It's part of our unwritten travel code.

I told him:

"Chor na b""d, chalte hain.""

We started to walk away, but realized one of our friends was missing. He had stayed back, got confused, and instead of backing us, turned against us for a moment — started yelling over the phone, scolding us like we'd betrayed him.

Later, he called again, this time calmer:

"Le jao saalon, kahan phasa diya mujhe!"

One of the guys arranged a bike, picked him up, and got him back. No harm done, just more laughs for the next day's retelling.

We rode back to the hostel, some on bikes, some walking. The streets were quiet again, like they had never seen any madness. That's the magic of Goa. It absorbs everything by sunrise.

Back at the hostel, the lights were dimmed. Some were still awake, whispering, smoking, stargazing.

I found my bed, threw myself onto the mattress like a man collapsing after a journey. The night had taken everything from me — and given even more.

Sleep came not as rest, but as a surrender.

And the next morning is unknown to me and would bring a new chapter.

Chapter 8

The Girl with German Eyes

The next day passed like it never existed. We slept the entire day — knocked out from the madness of Darling Bar, Diya, and all that unfolded. When we finally opened our eyes, it was evening already.

"Pandit asked me about Diya, probably expecting some romantic hangover from the night before. I just smiled, lit a cigarette, and said, 'You're talking to an emotionless Nomad, Pandit. I'm not a heartful or committed man. I don't hold on to people — I collect moments. I play, I move, I disappear when it's time. But one thing's for sure — I stay clean from the inside. No drama, no guilt, just flow but don't use anyone, be simple with you and your concept.

We discovered that the speaker we had wasn't good enough for the kind of night we wanted. Goa doesn't forgive weak sound. So, I and Pandit got up, still groggy, and took off to Mandrem to buy a proper sound system. Something that could shake a hostel to life.

We came back with a costlier setup — not for show-off, but for vibe-up.

By the time we returned, the garden had started glowing again. People were gathering — soft music, open bottles, lazy laughter. The party had begun.

As we plugged in the new sound, an Italian guy showed up — a bit creepy, definitely cheap in his approach, hovering without real presence. Still, the scene was calm. Varun, Paul, and Paul's girlfriend joined us soon. Conversations flowed again — this time about a new property. We were serious about it. It wasn't just talk. We were going to hire them, collaborate, and build something real.

Paul and his girlfriend showed genuine interest in our ideas. They respected the vision — and the vibe.

Varun, meanwhile, was in a different zone. Sipping beer, he kept talking about a German girl he was eyeing. He described her in detail — how he had noticed her, her energy, her movements. That was his focus for the evening.

Pandit leaned toward me, still half-smiling, and started telling me stories from the previous night. I listened, but all I said was:

"I don't carry emotions in intoxication. I'm a flaw person. A nomad. I don't have a destination… or attachments."

That's when she arrived.

A girl walked out casually — toothbrush in hand, still doing it. She saw the group, smiled with sleepy eyes, and said:

"Hi, everyone."

Varun's eyes lit up like Diwali. But we just nodded and returned to our drinks. She was stunning, yes. A natural beauty. Simple, clean, and powerful. A soft presence that didn't need attention — it earned it by just existing.

She joined us without asking. Pulled up a chair, brought her own drink. That's the rule of hostels — your drink, your vibe, your responsibility.

As the night rolled forward, Varun was full-on trying to impress her — spiritual talk, exaggerated stories, and some random fakery about meditation. Full fukrapanti. She smiled politely but wasn't buying it.

Instead, she slowly turned her focus toward us.

She introduced herself. Said she had been on a world trip. She was in Sri Lanka before India, and she had worked for PepsiCo on a good position. Now, she was simply traveling the world — funded entirely by her savings.

She was a dance lover. That was her soul.

I observed "People here aren't just traveling to see places — they're traveling to meet themselves. Free from labels, free from rules… just excited to explore the version of themselves they've never met before."

We played AP Dhillon's song — "Dil naal laale ni tu laare…" — and the vibe shifted again.

Varun said, "Explain this to her also."

We tried. But reality struck us — even foreigners are not great at English. They struggle just like we do. European, American, Indian English — they're all different accents. They may look confident, but they're not always fluent either.

She didn't understand the lyrics, but she felt the beat.

She stood up — and started dancing. Wild, beautiful, unfiltered.

I joined her. On the other side of the table, following the rhythm. Varun watched, jealous, but he couldn't do anything.

She liked it. Because I wasn't pretending. I was just in love with music.

After a while, she turned to me and asked:

"Who was playing the clap box last night? Was it you?"

I smiled.

"Yes. That was me."

"Please play for me. Again."

I picked up the clap box and began. This time with more energy, more connection, more fire.

While I played, she asked about smoking meditation. She had heard about it from someone else in the hostel. She was deeply curious about Indian culture and heritage — not just the commercial parts, but the spiritual essence.

And I thought: these westerners… they're more interested in our roots than we are. A time will come when they'll take it all, and tell the world it was theirs.

Suddenly, she asked again:

"Come. Dance with me. But on a German song. I'll teach you."

I agreed. She played something from her phone, showed me a few moves, and we danced. Not perfect, not technical — but full of soul.

People were watching. Some jealous. Some confused. Some smiling.

Then she surprised everyone.

She said, "I love Bollywood too… watch this!" and played "Chikni Chameli."

She danced so well — showing me videos of her school performances on the same song. I stood there, shocked, realizing how much the West admired our culture while we were busy ignoring it.

And I thought, I'm from Punjabi region. I must show her my roots too.

So I played a Bhangra track and asked her to dance my way. She followed, laughed, matched my steps. It wasn't just fun — it was magnetic. A blue-eyed girl from Germany dancing Bhangra with a desi nomad in a Goan hostel. Who writes this stuff?

We clicked. Like two frequencies finding their match. No layers. No filters. Just raw soul.

She was so simple. So beautiful. So clear. Like a girl from heaven who decided to travel on earth.

I felt something shift.

When two clear people meet, they don't crash — they click.

I looked around. People spend lakhs to feel what we were living. And we were doing it with bare minimum investment, just authenticity, music, and truth.

That night, something started.

And it wasn't just another party.

The party at the hostel was still on — some people had left, some stayed, and some just sat around, their faces clearly painted with jealousy or unspoken curiosity. But me? I was just enjoying. I wasn't performing for anyone. I was living in my own rhythm.

Now Pandit too had caught on — trying to impress Greta with his energetic dance moves. The same Italian guy, still lurking around with his creepy energy, started copying the same steps. The attention wasn't shared equally, and it showed. But I didn't care.

The talk of the night shifted — someone said, "Let's go to Shiva Valley." That place had become legendary. A 48-hour non-stop party right in front of the sea. No limits. No rules. Initially they charged for entry, but we had our own way. Foreign girls entered free, and if you had the energy, you didn't need a wristband — you just needed intention.

Varun wasn't in the mood to go. Maybe he was drained, maybe just not feeling the trip. But he made sure to send a few hostel boys to keep an eye on Greta — clearly still invested in her story.

So it was me, Pandit, Greta, and a bunch of others who were ready to go. And just like that, we headed toward Shiva Valley — no entry fee, no passes, just pure presence.

We reached as the sky turned orange — around 6:00 AM. The party house stood like a beast on the edge of the sea, facing the river. It was alive. The music wasn't fading — it was picking up, charging into a new high as morning light touched the waves.

I bought myself a drink. As I pulled out my wallet, Greta instantly paid.

No words. No hesitation. Just a gesture. Independent. Effortless. And I said — half-joking, half-serious:

"Indian girls should learn these manners."

We laughed.

We danced. The floor, the shore, the open road — everything was a stage. Greta was connected to her roots, wild but graceful. Not dancing to impress — she danced to express.

We drifted down toward the shore, where the music was still pumping. On the speakers came "Sheila Ki Jawani." Pandit, already in the zone, started calling himself "Sheila", doing funny moves. Child beggars, two of them, were selling night-lights nearby — glowing sticks and laser dots — but even they started dancing with her. No judgment, no gap between worlds. Just music. Just moment.

Suddenly, in the middle of all that, she hugged me — arms warm, her breath slightly shaky.

She looked me in the eye and said:

"Do you still feel like you're searching for a woman? I'm already in your hug."

She was intoxicated. Her voice was gentle. Honest or blurry — I couldn't tell.

So I didn't reply.

I smiled and thought in my head:

"Bache ke saath mazak mat karo. Ek toh engineer, vo bhi mechanical… upar se foreigner hug karke poochhe — still searching?". (*"Don't mess with the kid. First of all, I am an engineer — and that too, mechanical… on top of it)*

That day, I decided…

"Main ek sakht launda hoon."

Just then, Varun's hostel boys noticed the whole scene. One of them came running toward us, saying:

"I need a hug too. You're exchanging some next-level energy here!"

Even Pandit, in full Rajpal Yadav style, cried out:

"Mujhe bhi chahiye bhai, mujhe bhi chahiye!" ("I want it too, bro! I want it too!")

The scene was dramatic. I laughed, pulled them both in, and hug them and said:

"Shakal mat dikhana… mil gaya na!" .("Don't show me your face… you got what you wanted, right?")

They laughed but also looked a bit emotional. Greta hugged them too, spreading the same free energy without holding back.

Then she came back to me again.

Same look. Same question.

I didn't give an answer this time either. I just hugged her — slowly, firmly — and said:

"Feel the vibes."

And we stood there. Half an hour passed. No talking. Just presence. Energy. Clarity. There was no music needed after that.

Pandit finally broke the silence:

"Sari nasha utar gayi, chalte hain ab." (The high's gone, let's head out.)

I smiled. Around us, one of Varun's hostel guys stared with burning jealousy — like he could kill me with his eyes. But I didn't flinch.

I wasn't showing off. I was just feeling what was real.

Just then, a group of Germans arrived — Greta 's friends. They tapped us out of our trance and said they were waiting to say goodbye to her before leaving. It was almost 10 or 11 in the morning. The sky was bright now, but we felt like we were floating.

We decided to return. Something had changed. We weren't just walking back — we were carrying an invisible layer of vibes, attachment, and a little heaviness.

We reached the hostel — the lights were dimmed. Almost everyone was asleep, even the ganja boy beside the courtyard.

We didn't speak much.

We lay down in silence.

And decided to rest.

Chapter 9

Artjuna, Emotions & the Borrowed Love

After barely 2–3 hours of sleep, I felt a gentle voice call me out of the haze. It was Greta — standing by my bed, her wet hair dripping, the scent of shampoo mixing with the early sun and hostel dust.

"Let's go for breakfast," she said, like it was the most normal thing in the world.

I rubbed my face, half-awake.

"Good morning," I replied, though it was probably afternoon already. But mornings aren't about clocks — they're about energy, and I liked starting mine this way.

I called Pandit to join — he mumbled and denied.

So, I got ready and left with Greta .

We reached Artjuna Café again. And like every time, the vibe hit different.

This café in Anjuna is something else. Authentic food, bohemian crowd, banyan trees wrapping the space in shade — it's not just breakfast, it's a slow experience.

I usually don't eat early. My life is chaotic. Nomadic. No set routine, no balance. I often eat once a day — maybe around 5 PM. Fruits, juices, whatever I find during trips. But how could I say no to her?

After all, if you've ever had a mechanical engineer around, you'd know how messed up and magnetically unstable our emotional circuits are.you can understand if you have this kind of species around you, unique and everywhere found still endangered category.

Suddenly, I noticed something.

Almost all the guys from the hostel were following us — tailing us like a jealous army. Greta noticed too. Their eyes were loud, even if their mouths were shut.

And that's when she smiled, took a spoonful of smoothie, and gently fed it to me — right in front of them.

She pampered me without hesitation and whispered:

"This mindset… it's everywhere in the world."

The Italian guy, too, was among them, hovering awkwardly. I laughed inside. We finished our breakfast, sat close, and even held hands, just to feel the warmth — and burn a few jealous hearts.

After we left, we decided to explore the clubs of Vagator and beach shacks of Morjim. A little more Goa, a little more madness.

We headed out on scooters — me and Greta on one, Pandit and that Italian guy (Roman? I don't even remember his name) on another.

We reached Morjim in the evening, took a short bath in the sea, then grabbed shakes at a beachside shack. That's when the conversation turned… personal.

It started with a simple topic — life partners.

Greta told me that back in Germany, she was in a relationship. But now she lives with her mother, post-breakup, and is just exploring, healing, flowing.

Then she asked me:

"How do you see your upcoming life?"

I paused.

And for the first time, I noticed — Western girls can be way more emotional than Indian girls. It's not always what we think. Sometimes, they're the ones searching harder.

She looked serious — like she was thinking about us.

And I?

I replied honestly:

"I don't have plans. I'm just living the moment. Feeling the vibes. That's all."

I could see in her eyes — she wanted more than just the moment. Maybe something real. But I couldn't offer that. Not then. Not in two days.

"Two days main toh apni khoyi hui shocks bhi nahi dhoondh paata," I laughed to myself.

We walked on the beach under the first stars of evening, the ocean humming beside us. Somewhere behind, Roman asked Pandit quietly:

"Should we leave them alone... or should we join again?"

And Pandit — as usual — copied the same behaviour from Darling Bar night. Creepy, weird, unnecessary.

Bro, if you want to join — join.
If you feel they need space — give space.
But don't go asking, "Should we leave?" That kills the vibe.

Pandit knew it, and still did it again same locking in washrooms.

As we stood together, Greta hugged me tightly... and kissed me.

But I stopped her.

Not because I didn't want to.

Because I have a rule — play and live, but don't use anyone. And she was feeling something real.

I didn't want to blur her emotions just because of a night or a mood. So, I stopped. Gently. Silently.

We moved on. Toward Vagator for another happening night — some club vibes, dim lights, soft alcohol, loud beats, and a foreign-Indian cocktail of energy.

We danced. We chilled. Then we came back.

Back at the hostel, Varun was still awake. The group slowly dissolved. Everyone started getting to their beds.

Greta promised me she'd stay with me the next day and night. No parties, no crowd. Just time.

After she slept, I stayed up with Pandit and Varun.

We talked. Man-to-man. Raw conversations.

We talked about why boys don't fall in love easily, and how we end up believing our friends more than our own feelings. After all those talks, I started wondering — was I starting to like her too?

Maybe.
Maybe not.

I didn't know myself anymore.

But I knew one thing — these kinds of pushes from friends often become the reasons for sorrow later. The kind that ends with a drink in hand and an ache in the chest.

"But ch"* banne ki aadat hai… har baar bante hain."

(We're addicted to being fools. And we do it willingly every time.)

discussion was like this

Varun:

"Bro tu gaya… tujhe toh clearly feelings ho gayi uske liye."

Pandit:

"Haan bhai, dekha tha maine tujhe… jab vo tujhe hug kar rahi thi, tu hawa mein tha."

Varun:

"Yaar aisi bonding timepass wali thodi hoti hai, don't lie to yourself."

Pandit:

"Accept kar le, it's okay to feel something… tu bas dikhata hai tough hai."

Varun (grinning):

"She touched your heart bro, aur tu keh raha hai kuch nahi hua, aaj nahi bolega to pura life sochega?"

You (quietly, nodding):

"Haan… maybe." shrugs

"Bas samajh nahi aa raha… but kuch toh feel hua tha."

Still, I made a decision.

"Tomorrow, I'll tell her my feelings. Even if they aren't mine."

Yes. They weren't real. They were borrowed feelings.

But I was already past the point of logic.

That night, I slept not with peace, but with false love resting on my chest.

I broke my rule.

I became a soft version of myself.

I became everything I said I wasn't.

Chapter 10

Querim Beach — The Edge of Vibes

Next morning, after a long, deep sleep — I felt clear. Clear in my head, light in my chest, no hangover, no borrowed feelings. Just peace.

Some new faces joined us — Maya and others from the U.S. — adding their own color to the group. The plan was to explore Querim Beach, one of the most remote and untouched beaches in Goa, far from the noise, deep in the calm.

We stepped out for lunch — a small, authentic restaurant near the hostel. Nothing fancy — just the kind of place where real food is served without filters.

She ordered a fish thali, local and aromatic.

I, being vegetarian, went for my regular — fruit juices, coconut water, and something light. That's me — nomadic and imbalanced. I usually eat once a day, around evening, no fixed pattern. But with her, I adjusted.

Then we were ready to go.

She sat on my bike. Pandit said he'd join us later, probably busy with Maya — which he admitted later, grinning like a villain from a rom-com.

We left.

The ride to Querim was beautiful. Mandovi River shimmered on one side, tall green trees wrapped the road on the other. It felt like we were driving through a postcard. She kept resting her hand on my shoulder gently as we rode. No words — just wind and warmth.

Querim Beach was something else.

A raw, untouched shoreline. No cafés. No music. Just sand, sky, and waves. A temporary Maggie stall, a small changing hut, and silence — the kind of silence that heals.most beautiful place in goa.

We spread out a mat and sat down.

"Ready for the meditation you promised?" she said with a grin.

We closed our eyes.

I guided her — nothing formal, no spiritual drama — just breath, body, presence. Half an hour of stillness, with the ocean whispering nearby. She followed deeply.

When we opened our eyes, the sun had shifted. Time had bent. We'd both gone somewhere.

She opened the conversation, softly:

"Do you believe in God?"

I replied honestly, as I always do:

"I don't follow anything fixed. I just do what feels right. I've studied from many masters, learned from many techniques… but now I just pick what heals. What brings me home."

She nodded, deeply listening. Westerners go deep into this stuff — maybe deeper than us. It surprised me every time.

Then suddenly, she said:
"Let's go swim."
I told her I wasn't great at it — could float, kick, maybe survive — but nothing fancy.
She smiled:
"I'll teach you."
She changed into her bikini. And I lost my breath.

She wasn't just hot. She was divine. The kind of body that wasn't sculpted for Instagram, but for freedom. For movement. For joy.

We entered the water together.

She laughed, moved with ease, splashed me like we were kids again. At one point, she lifted me partially in the water, and I felt her arms around me — the weightless intimacy of two people floating close.

For a few seconds, we were locked — body to body, heartbeat to heartbeat — and I forgot everything, even the little swimming I knew.

Eventually, I pulled away and said:

"You swim. I'll stay on the edge."

She nodded, continued her swim like a dolphin — wild, unbothered, graceful.

I sat on the shore, letting the waves wash over my feet, watching her — knowing something rare was happening.

Later, we reached the changing room.

There was no lock, so I stayed outside.

She went in, changed — or so I thought.

Suddenly, the door opened, and she pulled me inside.

Her wet hair hit my face. Her arms wrapped around me like vines. And she kissed me. Hard. Hungry. Real.

Our bodies pressed. Breaths got heavier. Hands explored. Lips searched. Skin melted.

The air turned electric. She was all over me, and I was melting into it

We fell to the floor, on the sand, no sheets, no distractions — just raw foreplay, warmth, and two souls burning gently.

But then I stopped.

I remembered a story — of a driver in Himachal, who unknowingly got HIV from a stranger. A short mistake. A long regret.

I whispered:

"Not today. Not like this. I don't want to lose a beautiful memory to fear."

She didn't argue.

I handed her my shirt, as her clothes had vanished into the sand.

She wore it — and somehow looked even more beautiful in it.

We rode back. Quiet. Connected. No one said a word.

Back at the hostel, we walked in.

And all heads turned.

People stared — she in my shirt, hair messy, barefoot. She didn't care. Neither did I.

Pandit was sitting with Maya, laughing.

I slapped him on the back jokingly:

"Saale, bulaaya tha protection ke liye, yha khud leke baitha h."

He laughed, shocked, clueless.

She went to her bed to rest. Promised she'd join the party after 3–4 hours.

Meanwhile, the party had begun.

More people. More stories. More music.

I hadn't said anything to her yet.

That night was our last in Goa.
We were leaving for Chandigarh the next morning.
She returned to the party after a few hours — sleepy, quiet, still carrying my shirt.
I pulled her close, lovingly.
"Stay. Just a little longer."
She smiled. Stayed for a bit. Then leaned in and said:
"I'll sleep. But wake me if I don't get up in time tomorrow."
She left again. Back to her dorm.
The night continued. Drinks went long. Promises were made.
"Let's meet again."
"When life wants."
One by one, hugs were exchanged.
One by one, we all slipped into sleep.

Chapter 11

The Departure — Borrowed Love, Earned Solitude

The next morning, I woke up restless.

Not tired, not hungover — just a quiet unsettled feeling. My body was packed, but my soul wasn't ready to leave.

I looked around — the walls, the bunks, the courtyard, the leftover bottles and stories still lingering in the air. I didn't want to go.

I looked at Pandit, and casually said:

"Let's cancel the flight, yaar. Ek din aur ruk jaate hain." (stay for one more day)

But as always, Pandit was practical. There was work. There were timelines. He reminded me that this freedom came with a return ticket. I didn't push it again.

We packed our bags.

A taxi was booked. We were late, almost in a race against time. Secretly, I kept thinking:

"Bas flight miss ho jaaye. Ek reason mil jaaye rukne ka."

(Let the flight get missed… I just need one excuse to stay back)

But fate wasn't playing that game.

Before leaving, I pulled out my phone. Started making goodbye videos — of all those beautiful souls, each with their signature expressions, weird habits, unique smiles. I didn't want to forget them. I wanted their vibe frozen in pixels.

Then I reached Greta's bed.

She was sleeping — tangled in her bedsheet, tired, calm.

I bent down, whispered her name. She opened her eyes.

No words. Just a tight hug.

I smiled and said:

"Give me a signature remark for the video. I want something to remember."

She shook her head.

"No…"

"Please," I said. "It's just for memories."

She looked into my eyes and said something that hit harder than I expected:

"I'll come to Chandigarh. I'll join you there."

I didn't react. I just smiled. Recorded the moment in my mind.

And then… we left.

Outside, the cab was waiting. Pandit was calling me again and again. We drove fast. Time was choking us now.

As we reached the airport, I got a message — the flight was delayed by 1.5 hours.

"Ab toh miss hone ka bhi chance nahi."

I looked outside the cab window — one last time at Goa's sky, and silently said:

"Bye… with love. And everything I didn't understand."

I've been to Goa many times.

But this trip?

It was different.
Borrowed love. Stolen emotions. Genuine madness. False peace.

We landed in Chandigarh. Back to flats, jobs, messages, locked doors, and regular beds.

As I sat in the cab from the airport, a message popped up on my phone. From Greta .

"You made me feel very low.
Every moment you denied me.

You forced me to stay last night at the party even when I was sleepy.
This morning, you tried to record me when I wasn't ready.
I landed back in my head.
Everything shattered."

i didn't reply never after this.

I stared at the message, blank. Numb.

So that was it.

Everything I thought I was carrying… maybe wasn't real after all.

Hostel beds don't always confess romance always. Sometimes they only witness misunderstanding, and broken moments which was never in real.

I closed my eyes. No regrets. Just… truth.
And told myself what I've always known:
"I am fine the way I am. I don't need to change for anyone."

I know my biggest problem.
It isn't commitment.
It isn't love.
It's this — feelings don't stay with me 1 even if i want. broken relation travel faster then me for my destiny.

Even if I want them to.
Even if I try to hold on.

What feels real today fades tomorrow.
What feels intense becomes distant.

And what seems like love — often turns into nothing at all.

I am a Nomad — not just by location, but by emotion.

I am flawed, but honest.
I am clean, but cold.
I want to feel — but I don't stay in the feeling.

And this time…
I broke my own rule.
I borrowed love.
I broke my rule. I tried to feel.

And in return, I realized — borrowed emotions never last.

Chapter 12

Borders, Drones & Broken Confessions with Operation Sindoor

I was in Rishikesh, writing under the soft murmur of the Ganga and the fading memories of Goa. The chaos had passed, or so I thought. I had finally found some breath — until the call came.

It was Veda .

Her voice didn't tremble. Mine did.

"I'm getting married on the 11th."

That one sentence crushed the calm. Everything inside me collapsed. Not with sound — but with silence.

I didn't reply much. What could I say?

I hung up. Packed my bag.

And without telling anyone… I rejoined my duty — this time, on the Indo-Pak border in Rajasthan.

The landscape changed.

So did my heart.

Gone were the hostel bunks and beach bars. Now, it was sandbags, drones, artillery, and confusion. The kind of confusion where you don't know if it's war or peace, or if peace is just a lie we tell each other before the next missile flies.

I arrived in the middle of tension. The air was hot, thick, heavy — but not from heat. From expectation. From fear. From rage.

Because two days ago, something happened that changed everything.

A cowardly attack on tourists in Pahalgam.

Tourists. Innocent travellers. People who carry maps, not guns. People who walk with cameras, not cruelty. People like me.

As a traveller — it didn't just shake me.
It broke something inside.

Because I have always believed, always said:

"Every tourist destination should be treated like your parents. With care. With reverence. With protection."

But this?

This was a knife in the chest of our national soul.

I've been monitoring the situation. Two days. Sleepless. Angry.

And a question keeps stabbing me:

> "How can such an attack happen without local support?

How can a few thousand rupees buy someone's silence? Or their betrayal?"

It's not just an act of terrorism.

It's an act of national disintegration.

To sell your land, your people, your humanity — even unwillingly — is to spit on the idea of unity.

And then came the answer.

India retaliated.

Kamikaze drones struck Lahore.
Their air defence systems were shattered.
Precision. Power. No words. Just fire.

And I sat in a control room nearby, silently watching the report.

And I remembered…

Five years ago, I had tweeted:

"One day I will contest General Elections from Lahore. Not as a dreamer, but as an Indian who believes in truth beyond borders."

That day might come sooner than I imagined.

Not with hate.

But with the hope that we, as Indians, stop being soft when our blood is spilled.

Amid all this, I finally opened my diary again.

Because when the world around me burns, I write.

Because when emotions choke me, I bleed them onto paper.

So here I am — picking up where I left off.

The story of a flawed man, a wandering soul, who carried no companions to his next trip — only memories.

I never take people forward.
Only their moments.
Only their truths.
Only their unfinished conversations.

Because memories are the only thing that stay loyal to me.

In my brokenness, in my laughter, in my madness — they never leave.

I sit here now, on the edge of a possible war, with the thunder of aircrafts above and the vibration of drones below.

And yet, I am writing again.

Because this journey, this story — Unscripted Night — was never just about hostels, kisses, or firelit confessions.

It was about this moment too.

When love fails.
When peace breaks.
When you sit between countries…
And still search for yourself.
The sirens went silent.

After days of alertness, rumbling aircraft, and drone warnings, the Indo-Pak border finally calmed under the announcement of a ceasefire. A strange stillness settled over the land. But deep down, every soldier knows:

> "Ceasefire is only a pause, not peace."

And true to form, within just three hours, the promise broke.
Shells whispered across the desert air, mocking the ink of fragile agreements.
The uneasy calm was shattered by cowardice pak.

As I stood watching the horizon through my binoculars, the irony hit me harder than the sound of distant fire.

I couldn't help but think:

> "This feels exactly like my own ceasefire had been broken."

A few days earlier, when I had been sitting in quiet reflection in Rishikesh, I had received a call that changed my course.

Not from any commander.
Not from duty.

From Veda .

The woman who had once found a place in my heart without even trying.
The one whose every word felt coded, precise, trained, disciplined — yet carrying hidden warmth underneath.
The one who never allowed herself the luxury of attachment.

Her message was simple, cold, and final.

"I'm getting married on the 11th."

It wasn't said with pain.
It wasn't said for discussion.

"Just information. No reply needed."

The same way Pakistan had announced a ceasefire — not for trust, but for tactics.
The same way they broke it soon after.
The same way she had called me only to close the chapter before I could speak.

Both left me standing, wondering what had just happened.

As I stared across the no man's land, that same message echoed inside my mind.

My thoughts drifted back to those first conversations with her months earlier.

How two very different people — an emotionally reckless traveller and a flawlessly trained intelligence officer — had started talking, joking, trusting in tiny doses.
How we had bonded over incomplete stories, unfinished nights, unsaid truths.

She always taught me:

> "Some things don't need answers.
> Some things are better left unsaid."

I learned it the hard way.

As I stood by the sandbags, listening to the faint crackle of wireless reports, I remembered the last message she had sent when I left Rishikesh:

"Stay safe ."

It had comforted me then.

Now, in the middle of chaos, it became my only anchor.

I did not call.
I did not reply.
I did not try to rewrite what was already written.

This time, I let the ceasefire inside me begin.

Because I realized:

"You can't control broken borders.
You can only protect your own boundaries."

The ceasefire at the border had ended.
The ceasefire in my heart had just started.

" Vo jo mazhabi deewarein banakar napak ko pak kar rahe the,
Ye shayad vehm tha unka, ki vo mere Hindustan ko barbaad kar
rahe the.
Har pal hai yahan ke mast malangon mein, apne watan ke liye
mar mitne ka h fitoor,
Aur har ujde suhaag aur mere watan ke rakhwalon ke khoon ka
badla le raha tha…

Ops Sindoor.' "

" वो जो मज़हबी दीवारें बनाकर, नापाक को पाक कर रहे थे,
शायद वहम था उनका — कि वो मेरे हिंदुस्तान को बरबाद कर रहे थे।
हर पल है यहाँ के मस्त मलंगों में, अपने वतन के लिए मर मिटने का है फितूर,
और हर उजड़े सुहाग और मेरे वतन के रखवालों के खून का बदला ले रहा था...
'ऑप्स सिन्दर'। "

Chapter 13

The Message Under Mehrangarh

The night outside is blackout silent.
The type of night where even the stars seem to hold their breath.
The kind of silence where men stand ready to do anything — even sacrifice everything — for the soil they belong to.

In that frozen stillness, my mind travels back.

That day, I was leaving a hostel somewhere. The backpack over my shoulders, memories in my pocket, the road calling again.
The train shook quietly as I moved toward my next stop — Jodhpur.

I checked into Zostel Jodhpur, one of those rare aesthetic hostels where the design, the vibe, the people, even the air seems made for Nomads like me.
From the rooftop, the view of Mehrangarh Fort stood like an ancient warrior watching over the blue city below.
The evening brought a Rajasthani gala night — folk music, live instruments, and conversations under fairy lights with strangers who would be forgotten by morning.

These weren't the Rishikesh-style hostels with rigid no-drinking rules and silent mornings.
Travel hostels in Jodhpur have their own rules, their own chaos, their own peace.

It was there, somewhere between the sound of sarangi strings and my glass of scotch, that my phone buzzed.

A message.
From her. Veda .
The unfinished conversation had found its way back to me.
The pattern was always the same.

I'd write:
"How are you?"

She'd reply almost 24 hours later — duty first, always.
Her replies were short, delayed, formal, yet they pulled me back every time.
Even when nothing happened, everything happened.

Slowly, the conversation opened into talk of business ideas.
She was an export consultant, sharp, brilliant, knew things most people never touched in textbooks.
I didn't want to talk business.

The reason didn't matter.
I just wanted any reason to talk.

What she never knew, and maybe never will, is that I was carrying something heavier behind my calm words.
I started a coaching institute with three partners.
One left when we had just taken our first step.
Another promised me big things, made me invest everything I had, then vanished when the time came to deliver.

I had invested nearly one crore rupees, trusting childhood friendships, trusting loyalty.
Both betrayed.

Both left me standing alone.

I never asked for help.
I have never told anyone about this betrayal.

Not my friends.
Not my parents.
Not even my shadow.

I never went to my parents.
Never begged relatives.
I held it in.
Because this pain was my responsibility alone.

I never blame anyone for my scars.
My rule has always been simple:

"Everything that happens to me is because of me."

I tried to restart — not for money, but to build something for those who deserved better.
I wanted to set a new standard, a place for students who couldn't afford the madness of big-city coaching fees.

But destiny wasn't interested in my plans.

First year: Gross profits.
Second year: A loss of nearly fifty lakh rupees.
The exact amount I'd feared.

I have many ways to earn.
I've always been capable.
But I still search for something that would keep my NGO alive.

A business that would feed my mission:

> "To give opportunities to those whose only mistake was being born poor."

I know the pain of being unemployed.
The silent suffering, the nights lying in a corner staring at nothing, breaking under invisible weight.
As I once wrote in my notebook:

> "Woh ek band band se kone mein baithkar, saari saari raato ke imthanon ko paar karte hain.

Yeh berozgar hai saab… apne kal ki aas mein, apne aaj ko barbaad karte hain."

> "वो एक बंद बंद से कोने में बैठकर, सारी सारी रातों के इम्तिहानों को पार करते हैं।
> ये बेरोज़गार हैं साहब... अपने कल की आस में, अपने आज को बर्बाद करते हैं।"

With Veda, business was just the excuse.

I wanted the conversation.
The attention.
The energy.

I had never met someone who listened so completely.
She heard my shayari, my poetry, my philosophies.
Nobody had ever done that before.
Nobody had understood my unfiltered thoughts the way she did.

And in that moment — I felt it.

Not love, not obsession… just the magnetic pull of someone who feels like they fit.

Every guy says,

"My girl is different."

But I had never said that before.
With Veda, for the first time, I thought:

"This is exactly what I want. The qualities I searched for… they exist."

Slowly, slowly… conversation turned to more frequent chats.
I saw her talking with Akash once on a video call.
For a second, my heart sank.
I felt lost, like I was standing between two people.
But I observed. Calmly.
Akash had no depth. No purpose. Just bed-talk flirting.
I didn't confront.
I knew my value.

So I stayed, kept engaging.

And she found me more sensible, reliable, mature.

That night, in the beautiful chaos of Mehrangarh, we decided:

"Let's talk. Let's drink. Just us."

The journey that had once paused… started again.

Chapter 14

The Unethical Traveller - Who Doesn't Care, But Cares Too Much

The sky over the highway was a dull, lifeless grey.
Dry winds whipped plastic wrappers across the blacktop.
A battered SUV cruised alone on the open road, windows down, music low, engine coughing like an old smoker refusing to die.

The driver, tall, rough-bearded, rugged boots up on the dash, flicked ash from his cigarette out into the passing void.
His phone lay on the seat beside him. Silent. As always.
There were no missed calls. No messages.
And that was exactly how he preferred it.

Or so he told himself.

They called him many things.
Some admired his cold detachment.
Some feared it.
The ones closest knew the truth.

This was the man who "protected without claiming".
Who led without asking to be followed.
Who don't care about anything, fearless .

Even his enemies whispered the nickname that followed him from desert to mountain:

"Nomad Tosh – An Unethical Traveller"

Not long ago, fate had tried to stop him.

A government assignment had sent him from "Jaipur to a classified location".
The afternoon had been quiet. A roadside hotel. An empty parking lot.
Until a screaming SUV, out of nowhere, rammed full force into him.

The impact crushed him between steel and steering wheel.
His chest caved in as bones cracked like dry sticks under a heavy boot.
The blackness swallowed everything.

The doctors later said it was a miracle.
An entire month tethered to machines in an ICU bed.
Tubes snaking from him like mechanical vines keeping a dying plant alive.
Nurses whispered outside the door:

> "He shouldn't have survived."
> "That much trauma… no one comes back."

But he did.

When his eyes opened, he stared blankly at the cracked ceiling above his hospital bed.
No panic.
No fear.
Just a single quiet thought, over and over:

> "Why am I still here?"

There were no answers.
Not from the nurses.
Not from the gods.
Not even from himself.

The Nomad had never believed in destiny.
His life had been about movement, not meaning.
Hostel nights. Random faces. Unfinished conversations.
Not purpose.

But this time he was thinking for motive of life.

For the first time, lying broken and silent in that cold sterile box, he felt it:
The weight of others.
Not the fear of dying.
But the terror of what his death would have done to the few who quietly was with him in SUV.

He was thinking about the who is there who is concerned, and to live for each other and social system, is the ultimate aim of life. really life has the only mean, does it make sense to live for survival ?

all these questions deeply changed the narrative towards the life .

Weeks after recovery, he rejoined the only tribe who ever understood him:

"Pandit, Mahesh, and Nandu"

They called him up one December evening.
Plans were already made.
Destination: Rishikesh.
The place where sins floated away and adrenaline ran wild.
They arrived under freezing clouds and checked into a noisy budget hostel.
Pandit had dragged his oversized duffel up five floors complaining the whole way.
Mahesh argued with the manager over hot water timings.
Nandu tuned his battered guitar in the corner like he belonged to another planet.

The rooftop turned into chaos by night.
Cheap whisky. Blasting portable speakers.
Two lady solo travellers mysteriously joining the gang out of nowhere.
Hostel magic.
As expected, Pandit and a friend both shamelessly competed for one of the lady.
I said, " abbey bc this is for relaxing, what we promised, we are not doing any socialisation this time "
He said I will go for *fluctuationship*.
this is the time of close friends only.
pandit said same dialogue to me " next time jarur ", let me focus on hottest lady on the earth and he offered him a drink.

by seeing all this nandu tried by his art, sang a song for her .
but finally all over with broken hearts and empty night with
full of dreams and lot of laugh for me on them .
She ditched them both by midnight.
The Nomad stood near the railing watching it all unfold.
Amused. Detached. Unbothered.

> "Men never change."
The real madness began the next day.
They signed up for "24 km white-water rafting".
While others chose safer 9 or 16 km rides, he pushed:

> "If we do this, we go full."

The instructor eyed them doubtfully.
They launched into the icy embrace of the Ganges anyway.
The river showed no mercy.
Early rapids tossed the boat like a toy.
The sun vanished behind sharp cliffs.
Adrenaline replaced fear.
Then came the monster itself:

"The Three Blind Mice rapid."

On the third wave, the raft flipped violently.
Men plunged into darkness.

The water grabbed him with icy claws, spinning his body
like dead weight.
Underwater silence surrounded him completely.
Death circled, patient and indifferent.
But survival was instinct.
Years of learning kicked in:

"Lie back. Chin up. Hands behind head. Trust the current."
He floated up like a ghost resurfacing.
Saw arms flailing, bodies panicking.
Dragged Nandu by the collar toward the shore.
The guide pulled the others one by one.
On land, the instructor stared at them in disbelief.

> "In my career, I've never seen a group survive that flip intact. You were lucky."
The Nomad scoffed silently.

what i observe

The raft looked worn. Slightly underinflated.
"I don't believe in luck.
Only timing."
The group was shaken.
 "Bhai, get us out," Mahesh begged.
 "We can't keep going."
Nandu said " we will go on road by tracking, we will do everything but not rafting .
Mahesh and Nandu was grouping in side and saying to each other, don't get ready for further .
The Nomad stood cold, dripping, eyes sharp.
> "No way back.
> The only path is forward."

No one argued after that.

They completed the route because there was no other choice.

Back at "Shiva Hostel", the mood slowly softened.
The chaos of survival turned into celebration.
Nandu strummed wild chords on his guitar.

Whisky bottles clinked against metal hostel cups.
Laughter echoed through the corridors.

Videos of the near-death flip were shared proudly across dozens of WhatsApp groups before dawn.

Later that night, Nandu sat quietly beside him, staring at the floor.
Voice shaking and crying

"Bhai… I saw you drowning.
I thought you were gone.
And I panicked.
I thought—if Tosh dies… who will save us?"

he felt the feeling of nandu, he was thankful, that there is some people who will cry after him.

The Nomad didn't answer immediately.
Lit a cigarette. Watched the orange tip burn quietly in the dark.

Finally, with a faint smile, he whispered:
"I wasn't going to die.
Not today.
I never leave my people."

No one ever saw what lay beneath the surface.
They thought he didn't care.
He let them believe it.

But his rule stayed the same:

I don't travel for selfies.
I travel for stories.
Even if one day, my final story is my own."

May be i will not write that, but surely will give you some better and exciting end.

The conversations had reached their peak. Messages flew back and forth, ideas scribbled onto notepads, voice notes late into the night.
Handicrafts. Export. Potential. Plans.
Veda had spoken with the calm sharpness of a professional.

"No personal strings in business. Keep it clean."

But both knew this meeting was more than just business.
There were conversations left unfinished.
Questions left hanging between midnight calls.
They had to meet. Face to face.

Veda had just come off an intense assignment—PM security duty in the northern belt, where even breathing felt like a responsibility.
Finally, she had time.

So did he.
He needed air.
Escape.
A break from duties and routine that felt heavier by the day.

Aakash suggested Rishikesh over drinks.
They agreed before they even finished the second glass.

Somehow, they woke up groggy inside a packed sleeper coach, swaying slowly through nameless countryside.

As the train slowed into Rishikesh station, early morning mist rolled across the rails.
Somewhere nearby, temple bells began to chime.

A message blinked.

Veda : "I've reached early. I'm at the same hostel. See you."

The hostel was a familiar sight: simple gates, walls covered in fading graffiti, laughter and music leaking from the common room.
Backpack slung lazily over his shoulder, he walked slowly, calmly, but his chest tightened the closer he got.

Not fear.
Expectation.
For just one thing—that smile.

She stood casually in the dorm room.
Loose olive-green jacket. Simple black joggers. Hair tied in a messy bun that looked unplanned yet perfect.
One hand on her hip, casually talking with the hostel boy.
A girl who carried herself like the world owed her nothing, and she owed nothing back.

The dorm had shifted around her.
The messy energy of backpackers, clinking cups, hostel chatter… all somehow calmed where she stood.

And then she turned.
Her face lit up, and there it was—that smile.

The same smile that had held him steady through storms of uncertainty.
A smile that didn't demand attention but owned the room anyway.
It spread nothing but positivity and trueness, untouched by the noise of the world.
A smile that gave others hope without them even realising it.
Like sunlight cutting through cold fog.

But behind it, he saw what no one else could.
That smile was a curtain.
A delicate mask placed perfectly over the deep, silent grief that sat quietly in her eyes.
Eyes that held galaxies of unspoken pain and unshared burdens.
Heavy, tired, and honest.

"You fool everyone," he thought, standing motionless, "but you can't fool me."

The two seconds felt like eternity.
The noise of footsteps, plates clinking, someone laughing in the background—all disappeared.
The universe gave them that quiet second, frozen, meant only for them.

When her eyes met his and the corners of her lips curved just a little higher, he finally breathed.

"This meeting had to happen," he whispered in his mind. "For both of us."

Chapter 15

The First Evening Together

They walked in quietly, no drama, no hugs, just calm understanding between two people who had waited long enough to not rush.
Formal talk began the moment they dropped their bags.
Handicrafts. Export plans. Timelines. Samples. Logistics.

Veda had taken bed 103-B, tossing her small tactical backpack on the upper bunk like a soldier throwing down a kit bag.
He and Aakash picked random beds, shoved their stuff into rusted lockers, and locked them without a second thought.

The hostel air was heavy with that unique blend of dust, incense, and hostel detergent. Someone's bluetooth speaker played soft indie tracks somewhere in the common room.

"We'll talk more tonight," Veda had said simply, already pulling her hair back and tightening her boots.

There was no need to ask where she was going.
Duty always called her before anything else.

The door clicked shut behind her.

The boys got ready for the night ahead.

Aakash opened the rucksack where bottles were packed secretly like contraband.
The caps popped.
The sharp sound echoed like the start of a ritual.

The hostel was filling fast.
Saturday night energy.
New groups with loud voices and bigger backpacks arrived by the minute.
Laughter bounced from walls, hostel staff dragged extra mattresses across the floor.

The Nomad leaned back on the common room sofa, cigarette hanging lazily between fingers, eyes half-watching the door.

And then she walked in.
This time, something had shifted.

Her cheeks flushed slightly — soft, warm, unexplainable.
That blush.

A blush unlike any other.
Not childish.
Not shy.
But that rare Veda blush which only came when she wanted to say something, but pride held the words back.
A silent confession trapped behind a warrior's discipline.
No one else would have noticed.
He did.

The Nomad smiled faintly and said nothing.

The night started slow, just as planned.
They ordered food first.
Veda is foodie, she looks so loving when eat something.

She ordered Alfredo white sauce Pasta, and potato wedges, also pizza.
All was set to start
Nothing heavy. Nothing to break the rhythm of the evening.

She sat opposite him, picking at her plate with the innocence of a child focused on tasting every texture.
He watched silently, always observing.

There was a certain rhythm to her.
The way she explored food was playful, delicate.
Bite. Thoughtful pause. Next bite.
Simple joy.

And then he noticed it.

She reached for her seeper water bottle, twisted the cap in her uniquely careful way, sipped slowly, wiped the edge with the back of her hand and placed it back like a priceless object.

"So sweet," he thought, hiding a small laugh behind his drink.
"So Veda ."
The cigarette pack slid out of his pocket almost out of habit.
He tapped one loose.
As he lit up, she caught him.

Not a scolding.
Not irritation.
Just that look.

Her voice came soft, with a small tilt of her head and half a playful frown:

"Stop it, na. I will break it."

It was not the first time.
Not the last either.
She had said it a hundred times before, always with the same calm, lovingly.
Never angry.
Never demanding.
Just requesting him to care for himself, in her own gentle way.

He thought in her mind and spoke
This is why I smoke cigarette

" तू एक सिगरेट सी मिली थी मुझे,
कश एक पल का लिया और लत उम्र भर की लग गयी "

She smiled and broke my cigarette, even she doesn't have any problem if he will give this to anyone other, environment was not a concern

He smiled, flicked ash into the tray and replied softly:

But I do every time in front of her this, to listen my care from her.

The evening was only just beginning.
The rooftop was alive, buzzing louder as the drinks disappeared and the music took over.

The most common thing I noticed was that almost every table had "Ranthambore" whiskey placed proudly in the center. It felt like a party of like-minded Nomads and travellers.

The flames of the bonfire danced like wild spirits against the night sky.

Voices blended into a stream of laughter, stories, and half-shouted lyrics over the music.

Veda looked at me with curiosity and asked, "What do you think about your future plans?"

I sipped slowly and replied, "A nomad is everywhere... not just in travel, but in life too."

I knew she didn't want this vague answer. She was hoping for depth.

But I wasn't ready. I was living for the moment, not for a plan.

I knew very well I couldn't be stable, even if I desperately tried.

Suddenly, her phone rang. She got excited and walked a few steps away to take the call.

It was her family guru.

The conversation lasted for a few minutes. When she returned, she laughed awkwardly.

"भाई, घरवाले पागल हो रहे हैं, लड़के का अता पता नहीं है
और कह रहे हैं चार महीने में शादी कर लो।"

"Bro, the family is going crazy — the guy's whereabouts are unknown, and they're saying, 'Get married in four months!'"

I smiled and teased, "Maybe someone is nearby and you're just not noticing him."

She shook her head, strict and logical as always.
"No. There's no one."

I paused, then asked quietly, "What do you think about me?"

She smiled softly but firmly.
"I like your company… but not that kind of relation. Because I don't think you believe in these kinds of attachments."

I understood. I knew I was only a moment, a memory.
Never the final destination.
Even if I wanted, nobody ever wanted me for long.
People enjoyed my presence in their journey, but never as a permanent chapter.

Still, I had to ask the question that had burned inside me for days.

"Who was he… the one you were texting late that night with so much excitement?"

She looked at me, a little surprised.
"Oh, you noticed?"

I nodded. "I wanted to ask but waited to meet you first."

Her face darkened slightly as she spoke with quiet pain.
"He is the hero of my life. We wanted to marry. He still wants to marry me.
But we can't… because we belong to rival families."

Her voice cracked a little. "Leave it…"

I nodded, understanding her grief, and thought to myself:

I will never be possessive. I want her to have her freedom.

But somewhere deep inside, I wished that I could have been her first choice.

In my heart, I whispered my poetry:

"बस इतनी सी ख्वाहिश थी उसके दिल के कोने में एक छोटा सा घर बनाना,
फिर चाहे झोपड़ी उसके दिल में छोटी हो, या कोई मेरा वहाँ भी पड़ोसी हो,
पर खोले वो दरवाजा दिल का तो मेरा घर दिखाई दे,
खुशियों में चाहे ना आऊं याद, पर उसे ग़मों में मेरा कंधा और अपना
सर दिखाई दे।"

Suddenly, the mood changed.

Preet, a girl sitting nearby, came over and unexpectedly hugged me.

"Superb, my darling!" she shouted drunkenly.

Veda quickly pulled her away and said coldly, "He's uncomfortable."

Akash laughed from behind. "Ohhh… jealousy!"

Veda ignored him and muttered, "She can spoil our table."

The music suddenly blasted louder. The party shifted into full madness mode.

A Haryanvi beat started playing loudly between English tracks… "Russian Badana".

Veda jumped in excitement and began dancing wildly under the open sky.

I just stood quietly, watching her.

That free spirit…
That same Veda who belonged to no one yet gave warmth to everyone.
The girl who smiled through her pain and danced as if nothing else mattered

The Nomad stood slightly apart, eyes fixed across the crackling fire.
Veda was there—casual, relaxed, speaking to a circle of strangers.
Her ease among unknown faces always intrigued him.
But something stirred inside.
Not possessiveness, just a quiet urge to reclaim what was theirs.
She was much involved and too faster to get the information about others.
She involved in them too much within few minutes .

He leaned toward Akash, voice low and sharp.
"We're pulling a Pandit-style rescue. Let's execute."
Akash gave a sly grin, understanding instantly.
But this wasn't Goa, and the crowd was bigger.
More unpredictable.
The same Goa trick wouldn't work here.
"We adapt," the Nomad muttered.

The plan began.
Akash moved first, stepping boldly into the group gathered around Veda .
He singled out one guy who stood too close, too comfortable.

"Bhai… careful," Akash warned.
"That guy standing near the fire is from a very big political family.

Best not to interfere between him and his friend. He's dangerous when angry."

The guy blinked, eyes widened just enough to hesitate.
Within seconds, subtle panic spread.
The boys quietly stepped back, retreating to other corners of the rooftop, leaving Veda alone.

The Nomad smiled inwardly.
No confrontation.
No scene.
Just a clean reclaim of space.
A move that even Veda wouldn't fully understand until maybe someday, reading this chapter.

Veda drifted back toward their side of the terrace.
"Come, sit here," the Nomad said casually, patting the empty mattress beside him.
She laughed lightly, shaking her head.
"You should just go with the flow.
Enjoy whatever you have right now.
I'm good where I am. Let me feel this vibe."

He nodded, understanding the unspoken boundaries.
No expectations.
No demands.
Just presence.

Minutes later, she excused herself to the washroom.
The Nomad lit a cigarette and stared at the flames.

Suddenly, footsteps approached.
It was Preet from the girls' group.

Her cheeks flushed, voice soft but slurred from too many drinks.

"Is she your girlfriend?"

He exhaled slowly.

"No. We're just friends. Business partners… maybe something more like understanding. But nothing like that."

The girl smiled faintly, her gaze distant.

"I want you to be mine."

The words hit him harder than expected.

A strange mix of surprise and awkward sympathy.

She was young. Drunk. Lonely.

And he understood what low moments did to people.

He answered calmly.

"We'll talk in the morning.

Let me take you to your bed first."

The hostel corridors were silent and dark, lit only by emergency bulbs.

He guided her gently toward her dormitory bunk.

Helped her sit, unlaced her shoes, placed them neatly beside her bed.

As she swayed tiredly, she leaned in for a hug.

He didn't pull back.

"A hug is always good energy," he thought.

"A clean gesture. A safe gesture."

He gave her the hug she sought—not as romance, but as warmth.

As a human moment between two strangers needing kindness.

She curled into her blanket without another word.

The Nomad closed the door softly behind him and walked back up the stairs to the terrace.

The night hadn't ended yet.

Veda was already back by the fire, waiting.

They shared a glance that said everything and nothing.
The conversation resumed as if no interruption had happened.
The rooftop world spun on.

The conversation shifted.

From work to life, from business to random philosophies.

The easy flow of words that only happens when two people know they can trust the silence between them.

Veda had suddenly grabbed his phone, scrolled through, and called a few of his close friends.

"Come join us na… we're sitting on the rooftop!" she laughed into the speaker.
 "Your friend is being too serious again."

Her energy was playful yet natural.
No hidden intentions, no hesitation.
She simply wanted to become a part of his world, to blend into the wild mess of friendships and life he carried with him.

He sat watching her, quietly fascinated.
There was excitement.
There was an odd pull.
Not the artificial attraction he had experienced countless times before.
This was different.

His friends often joked:
The Nomad had "a strange problem with his eyes".
If he looked at someone too long, they got drawn in, without him even trying.

But with Veda, he didn't do anything.
The connection built itself
Nomad asked "Veda tell me your body count, after all we all are traveller by soul "
She smiled and said "I don't know when it was last, but till today may be three or less "
And she said, tell me yours.
He was not expecting this question in return,
He replied, "I can't count my body count "
It was a stupid answer but still he can't say anything else.
There was something in her gaze that invited trust, something in her voice that disarmed even the strongest walls he had built inside.
She stood up suddenly, brushing invisible dust from her cargo pants.

> "Let's go to Sai Ghat," she said.
> "It's late… perfect time to feel the vibes."

He smiled faintly.
He knew what she really meant.
A chance to steal some quiet time.
A selfish little escape from the noisy rooftop crowd.

> "Sure," he replied.

As they moved, Akash, ever the third wheel, stood up too.

> "I'll come along."

There was a slight pause.
Veda's expression froze for a half-second.ae
Not rude.
Just faintly embarrassed.
The magic of the moment had been diluted.

The three walked back to the dorm floor.
The plan fizzled quietly.

Minutes later, Veda shrugged casually.

> "Leave it. Now mood is off. I'm not going."

The Nomad gave a knowing nod.
No push.
No persuasion.

He told Akash:

> "You go back to rooftop. I'll be back after some time."

Then he walked slowly to the dorm.

Inside, the yellow hostel bulb buzzed faintly.
Veda was lying comfortably on "bed 103-B", her hair loose,
scrolling something mindlessly on her phone.

He laid back on his own bunk just across, staring at the
cracked ceiling.

They talked.
Random stories.
Life.
Small jokes.
Quiet questions neither had asked on the rooftop.

He finally asked, softly:

> "Why did the mood change?"

There was silence.
The rustling of the sheets.
Then she stood, crossed the narrow space between them, and without a word, hugged him tightly.

Not a casual hug.
Not a friendly gesture.
A deep, long, wordless embrace that spoke of things neither of them had dared say out loud.
The kind of hug that feels like home after wandering too long.

A warmth neither had expected, yet neither resisted.

For a rare second, even The Nomad—the man who never let anyone in—closed his eyes and simply let it happen.

The night had shifted.
Something real had finally taken shape.
And for the first time in years, he had no idea what would happen next.

Chapter 16

The Purest Moment

The world outside faded into nothing.
The walls, the noises from the rooftop, the flicker of yellow hostel lights—all dissolved into air.
Two souls stood alone in a quiet universe of their own making.

The Nomad had always believed that when two pure souls meet, when true energy flows between them, it is no less than a divine alignment.
A cosmic pull neither person controls.
Two halves recognizing each other across the randomness of life.

As she held him tightly, their bodies warm against the cold December air, he knew this was more than desire.
This was connection.
This was the meditative union of mind, breath, heartbeat, and skin.

Her kiss came first, soft and searching.
His followed, gentle but deepening with every second.
They fell into each other between the two hostel beds, the dormitory door still unlocked, the risk only heightening the intensity.

Without words, he messaged Akash from the phone beside the mattress:

"Guard the door. Don't let anyone in."

Akash, understanding, quietly complied.

Clothes slipped away, piece by piece, until they lay together as they had entered this world—in the purest form of being human.
There was no rush.
No performance.
Only exploration, touch, taste, breath.

Veda guided his hands softly over her body, sighing, whispering encouragements that made him feel as if the world outside had ceased to exist.

"Please, softer, go slow… yes, like that…"
"No one has ever touched me this way."

Her voice was breathless, soft yet urgent, breaking slightly with every wave of feeling.
She pulled him closer, as if trying to fuse two beings into one.

Time became elastic.
There were no clocks.
Only rhythm and movement, rising and falling like tides.

At one point, soft footsteps approached outside.
The Nomad gently covered her mouth with his hand, signaling her to stay quiet.
They paused, breath held, hearts racing.
The danger passed.
They smiled and without hesitation, returned to each other.

More people walked by later.
They paused briefly, then ignored it completely.
The energy had overtaken every other instinct.
They were no longer just two people; they were energy merging into one form.

By the time it ended, sometime close to 4 a.m., they lay tangled, silent, breathless under the thin hostel blankets.
The Nomad traced the small love bites she had left across his skin, tiny bruises of affection and wildness.
Each mark held memory, scent, texture—a map of the night engraved permanently in flesh and soul.

"These marks may fade from my body," he thought, "but they will never leave my memory."

The room held the lingering warmth of them long after their movements had stilled.
He inhaled deeply, catching faint scents still left on the pillow, a mix of her perfume, sweat, of skin against skin.
He closed his eyes and drifted into sleep.

Two hours later, at exactly 6 a.m., his eyes blinked open to the soft click of a laptop keyboard.
There she sat at the tiny dorm table, fully dressed, focused, calm, and back in her role:
The disciplined export consultant.
Reviewing documents, answering emails, managing her clients with the same honesty and precision she brought to everything she touched.

He smiled faintly under the covers.

"She's always about duty first. That's what makes her different."

Her dedication only deepened the respect he had already quietly built inside for her.

He rolled back over, the exhaustion pulling him under again. The next part of this journey was waiting, but for now, sleep reclaimed him.

Chapter 17

That café girl —bookmark in my journey

Next morning, sunlight crawled in through the half-drawn curtains and danced on the hostel floor. I blinked slowly, still wrapped in the warmth of the previous night. Everything felt still… like time had paused to let me breathe.

She was still asleep on her bunk, one arm hanging off the bed, her phone loosely gripped in her fingers. Her face was peaceful. No makeup. No walls. Just a woman resting from the battles she never told anyone about.

Akash was already awake, brushing his teeth at the corner washbasin like he was preparing for a board meeting.

"Let's shift to another hostel," he mumbled between gargles. "That one near Laxman Jhula with a rooftop river view."

I nodded, half asleep, half tempted. The idea of a fresh place, fresh walls, new energy always excited the nomad in me.

But then… I looked around. The cracked window. The scribbled dorm beds. That messy shelf where she kept her seeper bottle and wet wipes. The familiar chaos.

"No yaar, let's stay one more day," I finally said.

He raised an eyebrow. "You sure?"

I was. I didn't need to say more. Some hostels are just places. Some become stages for your chapters. This one still had a scene left to play.

And somewhere deep down, I didn't want to change the backdrop just yet — not while she was still part of this frame.

Later, as we sat in the common area sipping chai, she said casually, "I've spoiled all my clothes during duty. I don't have anything to wear."

I looked up. "So you want to shop?"

She nodded. "Yes, we need to buy clothes."

We tried searching for some branded shops in Rishikesh, but didn't find anything suitable.

"If you've got plans, we can move to Dehradun," she suggested. "There we'll find enough stores."

But it was already 2 PM and none of us wanted to miss the night's plans.

"Tonight will be a fantabulous party," Akash declared, already in the vibe.

Veda said, "I saw Priya in my previous hostel. If you say, we can call her."

Akash jumped in, "Yes, yes, why not?" Though he knew she didn't know about Priya's last conversation with me. If she came, Veda might fight with me, and ultimately a broken heart always needs a shoulder — and that might be him.

Even though Akash is loyal, sometimes he does things like this.

I replied calmly, "No need. We already have a good gathering here. Still, if you want, you can call."

"That's okay," she said. "It happens sometimes."

Later, we decided to go to the Rishikesh market. We hired a public taxi.

I sat in the front seat; she sat beside me. My hand rested gently on her shoulder.

She asked again, looking into my eyes, "What do you want? Are you serious about me?"

In the heavy crowd of autos and narrow streets, she asked three times.

I didn't answer. I didn't want to give her false hope before I became sure. But deep down, one thing was clear — I wanted her in my life, any way, any place. On priority.

Still, she carried too much pain in her eyes. I didn't want to give more.

She sensed it too and softly said, "You should take time. I will take time."

We reached our destination. She started looking for clothes.

Being 6 feet tall, very uncommon in Indian girls, nothing seemed to fit her. Finally, at one store, we found a few articles that suited her. She bought them and said, "Oh God, shopping sucks. I'm hungry."

Akash and I tried lighting cigarettes while she was in the trial room. She stepped out, caught us, and without a word, broke my cigarette.

We couldn't live long without smoking, but her constant effort was sweet. It was her way of reducing our bad habits without preaching.

Just then, a monk approached us.

"Give me some money," he said. "You'll be blessed."

Akash asked, "What will you do with it?"

The monk smiled, "I'll buy a cigarette."

I chuckled and handed him money along with one cigarette.

Akash looked puzzled. "Bro, you never donate money. Why now?"

I shrugged. "Because he was honest. I can give when someone's true. I don't support begging because it increases child trafficking and fraud. But that monk... he didn't beg. He asked."

Veda was quietly observing everything. Her trust in me was building.

She came closer and said, "You're very interesting. I think there's a lot more to know about you."

It was nearly five. We decided to head back to Café Shalom.

Later, we decided to go to Shalom Café, but it was already too late, so we cancelled the plan. Veda went back to the hostel for some food and urgent work, Akash wandered down toward the river, and I decided to visit one of my favorite places — Saffo Café on Laxman Jhula Road.

I love that café. The food, the vibe, the calm chaos — it all sits just right with me. As I walked in, I noticed the usual setting: Indian espresso machines, wooden counters, and dreamcatchers dangling from the ceiling. I opened my laptop, planning to write my daily routine and maybe get some work done.

But then, the unexpected happened.

Two girls — probably the owners — walked out. Both were strikingly beautiful, but one of them immediately caught my attention. About 5'2", fair skin, brown eyes, and a naturally graceful aura with loads of humbleness. She smiled and said, "Sorry, we don't have a chef today. We can't serve food."

Disappointed, I sighed and my expression dropped. The other girl, equally elegant, stepped in gently and said, "But we can try to serve something if you want to have."

I smiled and said, "Give me whatever you can. I just want to sit here. I love the vibe."

They chuckled and agreed.

I asked for fresh juice, bacon, eggs — they didn't have most of it, so I said, "Serve me whatever you feel like."

They brought some local dishes and shakes. I loved it — the taste, the simplicity, the way they served with warmth. The younger girl, especially, was something else. Her eyes were like drone lenses — sharp, deep, absorbing everything. No makeup, no filter — just pure presence.

We chatted briefly. Nothing flirtatious, just warmth. She became my friend in those few moments. I, thanked her for her kindness, and promised to return again. She belonged to one of those rare moments you carry in memory — not because something happened, but because it felt right.

That café — that girl — became a bookmark in my journey.

Even later that night at the hostel, when food ran short and someone said we needed more, I instinctively raised my hand and said, "I'll bring it."

But my friend went straight to Saffo Café.
They weren't there.
But that place? Still held the vibe.

And that was enough.
Travel teaches you that there's more love in the world than we imagine. That's why I keep moving. Different people. Different behaviours. Graceful energies.

That's the magic of travel — every moment, every soul, every silence adds a new shape to who you are.

Chapter 20

Silent Heroes of Kupwara — The Jaish Faceoff

While I and Veda were sitting quietly on the rooftop that night, watching the stars and sipping slowly, something changed. She wasn't laughing like she usually did, nor teasing me with her mischievous smile. Her eyes had a different stillness — a depth that felt like it carried decades. I didn't say a word. I just looked at her and waited.
Then suddenly, without warning, she started speaking.

"There was a boy named Anil, " she said slowly. "He was with her in Srinagar… this was right after COVID."

Her voice had dropped — it wasn't shaky, just soaked in everything she had locked away for years.

"We were involved in a classified negotiation with Jaish-e-Mohammad. Some of our agents had been captured. We were sent in to secure their release. It was all going well until ego got in the way."

She went on to explain how a senior ministry official, who had tagged along for the deal, began objecting to his placement in the documentation hierarchy. He demanded his name be put above others. But the documents were pre-approved by higher authorities. This is the document in which hierarchy told them who is leading and to whom the other team members has to follow.

"That little spark of arrogance set fire to everything," she said, her tone still detached. "While we were trying to manage the situation, they saw the opportunity… and started firing."

It was around 3 or 4 a.m. The silence of the mountains was torn apart by bullets. It was a heavy firing.

"I saw Anil get shot. Three bullets. Head. He fell in front of me. He stepped ahead — to protect her. That was supposed to be me."

She paused, then added, "I got hit too… my knee shattered. Ligament tears. A long scar between my chest and stomach. Bruises everywhere. But I lived."

Their group had four people. Two were killed instantly. One went missing. Veda was the only one left, crawling for two hours through the rocks and the cold, hiding and surviving.

"My knee was locked. I couldn't even move it properly. But I had to keep going… had to stay hidden until backup arrived and also i have to watch eye and engaged them until backup arrived."

Eventually, she managed to flip one of the enemy informants and turned the mission around. She retrieved the captured agent and all Jem terrorist killed, but lost two of her own sources in the process.

Then came a different silence — the kind filled not with facts, but emotion.

"That night, before the mission… we drank together. Me, Anil, others. Around midnight. He told me he loved me. We trained together. He was my batchmate. He was the only son in his family."

She looked down.

"I didn't get a chance to say no. I wanted to tell him — that I couldn't, that Gaurav was already in my life. But I didn't say it that night. I thought I'd explain after the mission."

Her voice cracked. "But there was no after. He died to save me. Twice, he came between me and the bullets."

Her eyes were dry. But her words bled pain.

"I called him on that mission. He wasn't even posted there. I asked for him. And now he's not here."

After being shot and wounded, Veda lost consciousness in the dense forest nearby. Hidden between broken rocks and thick deodar trunks, her breathing faint, the night stretched endlessly. Hours later, a backup team finally arrived. She was barely conscious when they pulled her out. And with her evacuation began a second operation.

This time, they went in hard.

Within the next two hours, the backup unit tracked and neutralized eight Jaish-e-Mohammad operatives, including one of their key commanders who had been operating along the Kupwara line for months. The mission was successfully completed — but at a heavy price.

There were no tears. Just the echo of what wasn't said in time, of what was lost before it could even begin.

And I? I said nothing. I didn't interrupt. I just sat beside her and let her speak.

Because sometimes, people don't need answers.
They just need someone to remember the silence they carry.

But that was just one of the many stories she carried — stories that never made the headlines. Stories with no endings.

And maybe that's what shook me most — she had lovers, stories, and sacrifices all around her. So many who had.

I was left thinking — how do you love someone who is already carrying the lots of love and promises.

She once even shared a letter — written by another colleague during training. He had tried to end his life just to outperform her. Compete with her. Be above her. But later he realized Veda was right and he committed suicide and did all the property to her name, which later Veda. has not taken, but she showed me her last later, all was mentioned.

The one thing which i observed that intelligence and these operational departments carried a lot of pressure and have traumatized mind.It is too tough to live like these.

I was stunned. Because I'd only heard in movies that someone could die for love.

But here, with Veda — it was real. Too real.

And in all that chaos, I often wondered — who m I and how much does mean for her ?

Even now, I don't have the answer.
But I carry the question every day.

It was a scar — real and permanent.
A war story without medals.
A love that never got to become one.

And in that moment, I realized — she wasn't telling it to be heard.
She was telling it because she couldn't hold it in anymore.

And now, I carry it with me — not as a secret.
But as a truth too sacred to forget.

Chapter 19

The Silence That Broke Us

That evening, we went back up to the rooftop. The plan was simple — a calm night, soft music, and conversations. We popped open a bottle of Ranthambore, the most common companion on every table that night.

Akash began sharing tales from the previous evening, laughing as he recounted moments with exaggerated detail. Veda and I slowly slipped into our own little world, forgetting who was around. The rooftop faded into the background.

"I think no more drinks after tonight," she said, placing her hand over her glass. "It's time to detox."

I nodded. "I'm with you on that. After tonight, clean living. No more."

She smiled. "Anyway, duty's calling again in a few days. And I don't touch liquor when I'm posted."

For a moment, we forgot Akash was still sitting nearby. When he walked off to join another group, I gently hugged her and kissed her cheek. She leaned in, whispering, "Wait… time will come."

We started talking again, drifting into softer subjects.

"What do you like most?" I asked.

"I don't have big dreams," she replied, eyes steady. "I like tiny things. I don't want the whole world. Just a simple life. I wish to wear ethnic Rajasthani dresses… eat kathal someday. And Jaipur's dal bati churma — that's my favorite."

Something stirred inside me. I was drunk — not just on whiskey but on her words. I pulled out my phone, searched for cloud kitchens nearby, and found one that could possibly deliver in the morning.

"It's too late now," she said, laughing. "They won't take your order."

But I paid in advance anyway, insisting, "I need it all in the morning."

I even called Aryan, my childhood friend from Jaipur.

Our calls always began with colorful abuses.

"Saale, tu kabhi DBC (dal bati churma) ka fan nahi tha," he said after I explained. "We've spent years together and I've never seen you eat that."

"Bro, it's not for me. It's for someone special," I told him.

"I'll try to send it by morning. Otherwise, by afternoon in Delhi."

"I'm counting on you."

Back on the hostel rooftop, we heard loud singing from the Artbuzz hostel above. A group of girls were drunk, singing freely under the stars.

We laughed. Hostel vibes don't stay confined by walls. They're contagious. They travel — across rooftops, across hearts.

And just like that, we joined in from our own terrace.

One beat. One rhythm. One wild, open sky above us all.

That night, as I arranged everything for her — from cloud kitchen orders to long-distance food deliveries — I wasn't chasing love. I wasn't chasing her.

I was celebrating something far more fragile.

Her freedom.

The freedom to wear what she loves.

The freedom to talk her truth without judgement.

The freedom to choose dal baati over validation.

And while doing all this, a thought struck me — something I've quietly believed for years:

"When we fall in love with someone's freedom, we don't bind them — we build space around them.
And real love, if it must exist, should always come with space to breathe."

Most relationships fail not because people change —
But because they start expecting more than what was once enough.
That same spark that brought two people close, becomes the reason they burn out.

We often mistake closeness for control.
We kill the person's essence in the name of care.
We start asking why didn't you call instead of how was your silence?
We forget the version we loved was the one who wasn't trying to fit into our version of love.

So that night, it wasn't about me being good to her.

It was about me being true to what made us real.

Because in the end, she may not remember the dal baati.

She may not remember the guy who stayed up searching kitchens or calling Jaipur at midnight.

But maybe — just maybe — she'll remember the freedom she felt when she was with me.

And that...
That would be enough.
That night started like any other. We were talking again, lost in our world. I was sitting on one corner of the rooftop couch, and Akash was somewhere nearby—overdrunk, lost in his own zone. He had become almost invisible to us. Veda and I were deep in conversation, discussing business ideas, future ventures, and somewhere in between, pieces of ourselves.

That's when a man in a suit appeared, clean and well-dressed, sitting just a few feet from us with his group. He whispered something to his friend and then got up. He walked over—not to me, but straight to Veda . "Is there any hidden cafe nearby? Any offbeat spots to visit?" he asked casually, then smiled and asked, "Where are you from?"

I watched her. She responded politely, maybe a little too politely. There was interest in her eyes. Subtle, but there. Then the man said, "Sorry if I disturbed you."

And I replied, calmly but firmly, "Yes. You did. Please don't disturb us."

The mood shifted.
Veda turned toward me, her expression unreadable. Her body stiffened. Then silence.
Two full minutes of it.

Akash, clueless and drunk, stumbled back to our side. "Kya hua?" he asked. I explained everything, still processing the tension. I shouldn't have, but I forgot for a second that he was not just my friend but also my rival when it came to Veda .

In his attempt to fix things—or maybe impress her—he went over to those guys. I shouted after him, "Don't say anything. I can handle it."

But it was too late.

Veda got up. Angry. Scared. Embarrassed.
She thought I was ruining the vibe, that I was overreacting, creating a scene where there wasn't one.

"Your image was so high for me," she said, her voice breaking. "I was close to finalising something with you. But now it's gone. Crashed. I can't stay. I'm going to sleep."

And just like that, she left.

Akash came back, saying he had resolved the issue. Apparently, he had told the guy to apologise to Veda .

Then they stood outside her room, ringing the bell again and again.

Veda called me, thinking I was with them. Her voice on the phone was cold.
"Stop it. Let me sleep. Or I'll leave."

I was on the rooftop the entire time.

The guys came back.

Akash, trying to act heroic, said, "Now she'll come back to us. Let me go talk to her."

He went again, kept ringing the bell.

When she finally opened the door, she was on a video call with someone. A guy.
And then Akash—still drunk, still foolish—said, "C#### h kya hum jo yahan akela baithe hain?"

The words hit the silence like a slap.

I rushed down hearing the raised voices.
As I stepped in, she shouted at me. Her eyes full of fury. Betrayal.

The guy on the video call was on the bed.

My heart sank.

She was done.
"Everything's because of you," she snapped.
"Akash is innocent. You pushed them to act like this. I can't take it."

I wanted to explain. I tried. But it didn't matter anymore.
I was the criminal.
Everyone else? The jury.

I told Akash to back off, but he was lost. His eyes were dark. His mind not in the right place. He stared at her in a way I didn't like. It made me feel sick.

I walked away. Climbed back into my bunk. I didn't sleep. I couldn't.

I just lay there, texting her again and again.

She didn't respond.

And then the message came:

"I've booked a taxi. I'm leaving. We won't meet again. Goodbye."

One last time, she came to the room.
She hugged me.
A hug that didn't feel like warmth.
It felt like a door closing.

I whispered, "Please don't go."

She didn't answer.
She turned. Walked away.

I stood there.
Still. Empty.

The hostel didn't feel like the same place anymore.

We were both supposed to go to Delhi that morning.
But she left alone.

And I stayed back, with nothing but echoes in my ears and her perfume in the hallway.

It was over.

Just like that.

Like it had never begun.
Like it was never meant to stay.

Chapter 20

The Parcel That Carried a Heartbeat

The morning began with silence—not the peaceful kind, but the kind that screamed in your chest.
It was all broken. Shattered. Twisted like an unfinished line in a letter left on a page.

I had never known what real goodbyes felt like—until now.
This wasn't how people were supposed to leave.

I wasn't ready.

I had been the one walking away from people in the past—sometimes with guilt, sometimes numb. But this time, someone walked away from me. And they took something with them I hadn't known I had given—"hope".

There was an echo inside me. My mind? A maze of blurred thoughts. And as we packed up that morning, I kept thinking—

> ""Koi kitna bhi sakht launda ho… jab ladki aaye tab pighle na pighle, lekin jaane pe zaroor pighalta hai.""

And damn, that's true.

The masculine world never trains us to deal with exits. We toughen ourselves to resist falling, but nobody tells you how to stand when someone walks out without looking back. It isn't the girl coming in that makes a man emotional—it's the girl leaving silently, with no goodbye strong enough to hold.

And I decided—I wouldn't let her go that easily.
Not without one last try.

I still had doubts. Was she in intelligence? Her behavior had too many shadows and silences. I had asked her once, *"If you're in intelligence, Veda can't be your real name, right?"*
She smirked. "Maybe."
And that *maybe* messed with my head more than any straight-up lie could.

I even reached out to an old contact. "Check if there's anyone by her profile in active postings."
The answer came back clear—"negative". But suspicions are like cigarette burns: small at first, but they leave scars you keep noticing.

Then came Delhi. A meeting. Some old friends. But more than that—"a reason".

My friend from Jaipur called. "Bhai, ek parcel bheja hai bus se. Kashmiri Gate se uthana. Zaroori hai."

I knew what I had to do.
"That parcel—I'd give it to Veda ."
My last gesture. One last heartbeat delivered in cardboard.

And now, welcome to "the irony chapter of my life":
"Delhi. Kashmiri Gate. March. Pollution. Madness."

I called the bus guy:
"Platform 5, Kashmiri Gate par aayegi?"
""Haan haan bhaiya, 5 number platform par hi." Time 5:30 PM."

Easy, right?

Wrong.

I reached Kashmiri Gate, got lost in the chaos of luggage, chaiwalas, and honking buses from 17 states. I fought my way to "Bus Stand Platform No. 5", panting, limping with pain from an earlier injury.

I asked the bus conductor again.

"Bhai, yehi bus hai?"
"Nahi bhaiya, Metro Gate No. 5 bola tha driver ne. Wo doosri side par hai!"

"Wait. WHAT?!"

In Delhi, "Platform No. 5 of Bus Stand" and "Gate No. 5 of Metro Station" are two very different planets.
Separated by crowd, confusion, two escalators, a subway tunnel, three paan vendors, and a couple of existential crises.

I had "five minutes."
I was already injured. I had barely slept. And now I had to "sprint through Old Delhi like James Bond with a limp."

I ran.
Dodged a guy selling underwear. Almost tripped on a little kid's balloon.
Got hit by a swinging backpack.
And somewhere between a chhole bhature stall and a sutta corner, "I fell".

Hard.

The pain shot up my leg. It was the same foot. Probably a hairline fracture now. But I didn't stop.

Why?

Because "the heart doesn't limp" even when the foot does.

By some miracle, I reached Gate No. 5 of the metro— sweating, broken, breathless. And guess what?
"The bus was late."
By "1 hour and 30 minutes."

Of course.
Of *course* it was.

I waited. In pain. Surrounded by honking buses, with people asking "Jaipur? Jaipur?" every five minutes like a broken record.

It was "torture". Not just because of the foot, not just because of the pollution, but because I knew—"this parcel wasn't just paper and packing".

It was the last piece of me I could still send to her.

Finally, it arrived. I handed it to the bus guy with her Gurugram address. Told him it was important. More than he'd ever understand.

I didn't get to see her.
I don't know if she smiled, or cried, or threw it away.
But I sent it anyway.

Because sometimes, "closure isn't a conversation. It's a parcel you send in silence."

Chapter 21

The Handler, the Call, and the Truth

After Delhi, everything went quiet.

No calls. No texts. No accidental updates on social media. It felt like everything that had once moved in rhythm had now paused in mid-air.

I attended my meeting, caught up with some old friends, and came back home. But something within had shifted. Conversations around me felt hollow. Even laughter had lost its weight.

It was done, I thought.
Over. Buried.

But then—days later, in the middle of a dull evening—my phone rang.
Unknown number.

A soft, trembling voice broke the silence.
"Hey Nomad… Veda this side."

I froze. Not just because she had called after all this time, but because her voice didn't carry emotion—it carried "urgency".

"I need your help in Rajasthan," she said. "There's a source of mine in Pushkar. Some sensitive papers. They need to be delivered to the nearest police station. I trust only you to manage this quietly… it's a matter of national security."

There was no flirtation. No nostalgia. Just a straight mission brief.
I didn't even ask questions. Somewhere inside, my trust in her was still intact—wounded maybe, but alive.

I couldn't go myself—my foot was still healing from Delhi. So I called a close friend in Ajmer. A guy who'd shared hostel rooms and late-night bike rides. A guy who owed me nothing but had always stood by me.

I explained the task.
He paused. "Wait… you want me to go to a police station? With anonymous documents? Bhai, I already have a criminal record!"

I laughed lightly and said, "You're not doing anything wrong. It's for the country."
And after a long pause, he replied, "Every man has a place in his heart for the nation."

He agreed.

He picked up the envelope and went to the nearby police station.

That's where the situation changed.

The moment he handed it over, the questioning started.

"Who gave this to you?"
"What's in it?"
"Who are you?"

He panicked and called me instantly.

"Bhai, tune to mujhe phasa diya. They're asking me who my handler is!"

Handler. That word echoed.
Was I part of something… bigger?

The officers took his phone. They called me.

"Where did this packet come from?"
"How do you know the source?"
"Don't move. We're dispatching a team to your location. This document is too sensitive to be in civilian hands."

I froze.
So it was true. She was in intelligence. But maybe… "not working for us"?

My thoughts spiraled. Had I unknowingly walked into a real-life spy game? Was she even on our side?

I tried calling her. Switched off.

Just then, the landline at the police station rang.

The officer picked it up. His posture changed instantly.

"Yes, madam. Yes, Mrs. Dasy. Understood."

He stood upright, respectful. His voice dropped to formal tones. Within minutes, the conversation ended, and the entire room shifted. The tension was gone. They looked at my friend now with a mix of surprise and apology.

"You know Mrs. Dasy personally?"
"No, sir. I just did what my friend asked."

"Call your friend," they said.
When I answered, the officer simply said
"Sorry for the confusion. And thank you for helping the nation."

That was it, he does not explain anything .
That one phone call… had changed everything.

I sat there stunned. Dasy?
That was her real name? Or her code name?

She had never lied. She had just "not told the whole truth."

The next day, I called an old contact who owed me a favour. "Check a name in the selection list. I won't share it… but you'll know."

After a few hours, he confirmed.

"Yes, that name is in the list. Selected. Never officially joined. Possibly on an off-record and in any mission or did not join ever."

"Now everything made sense."

She wasn't just a mysterious traveller.
She wasn't a regular girl dancing under hostel fairy lights.
She was an "off-grid RAW officer"—silent, strategic, and embedded.

The entire story rewrote itself in my head.

She was telling the truth. She was never mine. She was never meant to stay.
She was a shadow, a file in a classified department, a soul trained to disappear and reappear at will.

And I... I had been a piece of her plan.
Or maybe... just someone she trusted for a moment.

I was shocked.
But not broken.
I was proud.
She wasn't some agent with foreign motives.
She was one of ours. Brave. Sharp. Dangerous. Loyal.

And I... I was just lucky to have met her without a disguise.

I sat there, stunned yet proud.
Not many can say they helped a RAW agent on mission mode.

I was in a state of quiet confusion—questioning everything. Was I truly connected to her? Was it ever real... or was I just a part of the mission?

Her life felt like a puzzle, and I couldn't tell if I was a missing piece or just a temporary move.
There were too many questions… and silence was the only answer I had

The irony? I had thought I was chasing a girl with a complicated heart.
Turns out, I had brushed shoulders with someone trained to disappear.

After all, she was in RAW. She had once told me that — not in a full confession, but a faint whisper of truth when we had been lost in conversation. For a long time, I was wrapped in confusion. Was I a part of her mission? Was I being used by them?
But even if that were true… it was for the nation. And for that, I carried a special respect. A deep, unshakable respect for the Intelligence of India. I had always assumed she worked in the analysis wing of IB. RAW? That was still a speculation… until it was clear.
A few seconds after all this storm, my phone rang.
It was from an army cantonment. A soft but commanding voice said, "Are you Tosh? Dasy wants to talk to you."
I froze. The line shifted and her voice trembled through.
"Sorry," she said. "I missed your calls. I was under attack. I can't share details. But I'm in the army hospital now. Safe."
My hands trembled. Heartbeat like thunder. Shock. Panic. A blur of emotions I couldn't even name.
She had mentioned missions before, in fragments. Casual mentions that I dismissed as stories. But this was real.
She wasn't just playing a role. She was the role.
And I — a mere frame in the picture she had to burn to keep her country safe

So this was my story — the one that wasn't supposed to end, but to begin.

I've lived many tales, met countless people, wandered through cities, and slept under stars. But never did I carry a relationship into my stories. They were always chapters that closed.

This one? This was a continuation.

Some stories are never meant to end — they are meant to begin.

And yet, even now, when I think of her, I don't see Mrs. Dasy.

I still see "Veda "—the girl who sipped coffee with me on hostel stairs and laughed like she didn't belong to the shadows.

She may have been a ghost in the system. But to me, she had always been real, But this time, the only feeling I carry

" अर्से बाद उसे देखकर, ज़रा दिल ने दम भर दिया,
और किया खंबख्त से बेपनाह, बेंतिहा इश्क़ इतना कि — सारा
इश्क़ ख़त्म कर दिया।"

(After ages, I saw her—and for a moment, my heart took a deep breath. And then I loved that wretched soul so endlessly, so madly... that I used up ended love itself all the love I ever had)

www.ingramcontent.com/pod-product-compliance
Lightning Source LLC
Chambersburg PA
CBHW062143150726
47991CB00006B/2158